Made in the USA
Las Vegas, NV
16 December 2020

13703417R00127

<u>ACKNOWLEDGEMENTS</u>

I would like to give all my gratitude to the Most High Amen-Ra for everything in my life. Secondly, I would like to extend love and appreciation to my family, especially the ones who stood in my corner when the odds were stacked against me, I'm forever grateful for everyone's existence. Big up to the whole City of Trenton New Jersey. Big up to my second home, Greenville, North Carolina… Moorewood Projects, Poppie we got this!

"Trenton-Made"

CHAPTER 1

The clock hanging on the hospital wall read 9:45pm. The dangerous thunderstorm terrorizing the city prevented a lot of family members from being present to witness the new life that was about to be birthed in to the world. The winds were so strong that its violent whistles could be heard in the hospital room. Heavy drops of rain poured from the gloomy sky and on to the windows as if its main goal was to crash though the thick double layered glass.

Nyla lay in the hospital bed with her legs spread open, breathing heavily. Beads of sweat rolled down her forehead. She moaned and strained with each attempt to push her newborn baby out of her womb. "Hurry up and get this baby out of me!" Nyla screamed.

She was surrounded by her mother Candace, her 10 year old daughter Tadasia, and 3 nurses. The doctor stood at the foot of the bed. "I can see his head", he said.

The doctor looked up at Nyla to make sure he had her full attention.

"Nyla, I need you to calm down, concentrate, and give me one hard push. You think you can do that for me?"

Nyla turned to look at her mother and daughter before looking back at the doctor. She nodded her head.

"Okay, I'm ready to push."

Nyla did the best she could to gain her composure. Candace held a cell phone near Nyla's ear.
"All you got to do is calm down and listen to what the doctor is telling you to do baby."

Nyla's baby's father, Real, was on the other end of the phone trying his best to coach her through.

Real was being held in the county jail for an attempted murder charge. His bail should have been paid two weeks ago but when it

was time to pay, his right hand man Young A was no where to be found. Real tried calling him several times but the calls always went straight to voicemail.

When Nyla heard Real's voice, she immediately became angry.
"Fuck you Real! If you really cared you would be here!"

Real and Nyla had what you would call a love/hate relationship, and right now it was pure hate. She hated him for not being there to support her while giving birth, and she also hated him because of all the rumors she heard after he got locked up about him dealing with different women.

"Calm down and focus on having this damn baby", Candace snapped as she grabbed Nyla's hand.

"Come on mommy push! Push!" Tadasia exclaimed in the sweetest tone.

Nyla looked into her daughter's eyes and immediately refocused.
"Ok baby."

Nyla closed her eyes, inhaled deeply, and pushed as hard as she could, squeezing Candace's hand as if she was trying to crush every bone.
"Aagghhh!" She screamed in agony as she pushed the baby out of her womb and into the doctor's hands.

BOOM! An extremely loud thunderous sound roared from the sky as lightning struck the hospital building, causing the electricity to go out.

Loud cries from the baby echoed throughout the pitch black hospital room.

Nyla panicked as she strained her eyes, trying to see through the darkness.
"My baby, where's...what's wrong with my baby!"

"Relax Nyla, he's right here", the doctor assured her.

The doctor placed the baby on her stomach and guided her hands to touch him. Candace dug in her pocket and pulled out a lighter. FLICK! The fire from the lighter gave the pitch black room a reasonable amount of light, just enough to allow every one to see what was going on.

A feeling of relief came over Nyla when she looked down to see her son resting on her. The doctor and nurses used what little light they had to attend to the newborn, suctioning out his nose and mouth.
"We have to cut the cord and deliver the afterbirth", the doctor stated in a low tone to one of the nurses.

Just then all of the lights came back on, giving the room its original brightness.

Everyone gave a sigh of relief. The doctor cut the cord and did some assessments while the baby rested on his mother's belly. The baby

was then taken across the room to be wiped down and weighed. Nyla looked at Tadasia and smiled.

After wrapping the baby in a blanket, one of the nurses carried him back to Nyla and placed him in her arms.

"Aww, look at my little man", Nyla smiled as she took her newborn son into her arms.
"His ears are dark Nyla, he's going to be dark just like his daddy", Candace said.
"Mom, what's my little brother's name?" Tadasia asked while wiping sweat from her mother's head.

Nyla looked at her beautiful daughter and replied, "His name is Real."
"Just like his dad, huh mom."
"Yup!" Nyla nodded her head.

Meanwhile, Real Sr. began to worry after he dialed Nyla's cell phone number for the fifth time. *Why the fuck she ain't picking up the phone? Man something must have happened*, he

thought. He tried his best to keep calm, but couldn't.

"Fuck!" Real yelled, slamming the phone on the hook.

All the inmates watching TV in the day space quickly turned their attention to Real. Real didn't pay the onlookers any mind as he stormed into his cell, slamming the door behind him. His bunky was on the top bunk reading a book when Real came in.

"What the fuck is going on with my lady and my li'l man? Why the fuck am I still sitting in this shit hole?!"

Real kept pacing back and forth in the two-man cell. His blood was boiling and truth be told, he felt like beating the brakes off someone. Big Real stood six foot three and weighed two hundred and thirty pounds solid muscle, so it definitely wouldn't be a hard task to complete.

Good thing his bunky, J-Boy, was someone he knew from the street, or it would have went

down. J-Boy wanted to ask Real what was wrong, but when he glanced at him and saw the crazed look on his face he told himself to wait until he calmed down.

Minutes later, Real finally sat down on his bunk. He rested his elbows on his knees and placed both hands on top of his head as he stared down at the floor.
"Man, this some bullshit!"

That was J-Boy's cue.
"What happened bruh?"

Real stood up and turned to face J-Boy.

"My baby mom was in the middle of labor and the fucking phone hung up. I called back at least five times and the shit ain't even ring. I'm not even supposed to be in this shit hole!"

Real started raising his voice as he bashed his fist into the palm of his hand.
"I'm supposed to be at that fucking hospital with my family! My bail was supposed to be paid a week ago! This dizzy ass Young A

trying to play me for a sucker! He better pray to God I don't make it out of here."

The whole time Real was venting, J-Boy was pondering what to say to him. He knew Young A wasn't the type to leave a nigga for dead in jail, especially not Real. He loved him as if he was his big brother. J-Boy felt as though Real knew it too, and was just speaking out of anger.

"Big bro calm down, I'm almost sure ain't nothing go wrong with your lady and your son. The thunderstorm probably fucked up the reception on the phone. Just wait a few more minutes then try to call back."

J-Boy stopped talking for a few seconds and just stared at Real. He could tell by his facial expression that he was taking heed to what he was saying, so he tried to switch the subject. "I just can't see Young A leaving you for dead bro. He a good nigga. Something fucked up had to happen. You know how them streets can get."

Real frowned his face, "The only fucked up thing that happened was me not being able to see my son come into this world. You can't replace moments like that my nigga."

J-Boy nodded his head, "Yeah, you right."

"If Young A wanted to holla at me he know how to contact my peoples. He probably out there chasing after one of them dizzy ass hood rats."

Twenty minutes later Real banged on the cell door. "C O, open B5!"

The CO, who sat at his desk in the day space, called up on his walkie-talkie and told the officer working in the bubble to unlock the door. As soon as the door unlocked Real rushed out of his cell towards the phones. He grabbed the phone and wiped the mouth piece off with the sleeve of his bright orange jumper before putting it to his ear to call Nyla.

"Hey son, what took you so long to call back?" Candace asked joyfully after the call was accepted.

"I did call back but it went straight to voicemail", Big Real told her feeling relieved. He could tell by how happy Candace sounded that everything was fine.

"Oh, that was probably when we had the blackout."
"I knew something crazy had to happen. So is everything alright? Where's Nyla and the baby?"
"Nyla is sleep and I'm holding the baby in my arms. He's going to have dark skin and curly hair just like you."

A wide smile slowly spread across Real's face. That's all he needed to hear, he was good for the rest of the night.

"Well Candace, I don't want to be the reason Nyla wakes up, I know it's been a hard night for her. I'll call tomorrow morning when I think she's up."

"Alright son, I love you."
"I love you too."

After Real hung up the phone, he dialed Tee Tee, his little young thing he was dealing with on the side. Not only did she think she was his number one, and naive to Nyla and their new son, but she was pregnant by Real also.

"I miss you so much how's your day going?" Tee Tee said after accepting Real's call.
"It's going aight. Did you see Young A?"
"Yeah, I saw him earlier today. He rode pass me with some light skin girl in the car."

I knew it, Real thought to himself. "Why you ain't flag him down?" He interrogated.
"I beeped the horn, but he kept driving."

"Count time! Count time!" The CO announced.

The CO got up from his seat and walked behind the gate to lock the inmates in to their cells. The tier became noisy. Cell doors were being slammed shut, while majority of the

inmates were yelling to fellow inmates across the tier. Real put his hand over his ear so he could hear.

"Listen, remember that big white house on Edgewood you dropped me off at a few days before I got locked up?"
"Yeah, I remember", Tee Tee replied.
"That's Young A's girl house. I want you to go over there around 12 o'clock tonight and find out what's going on with my bail. Alright baby, it's count time. I'll call you early in the morning. I love you."

Real hung up the phone and darted into his cell where he got undressed, hopped in to his bunk and took it down for the night.

The next morning Real's eyes slowly opened after hearing his cell door open. He turned around and saw the same CO that was working last night's shift standing in the door way.
"Are you Mr. Johnson?" The CO asked.

Real nodded his head.

"Hurry up and pack your things, your ride is outside waiting on you."

Real dove off of his bunk and put on his orange jumper. *I wonder who the hell came up here to pick me up. If it's Young A I still want action, fuck that!* Real thought to himself as he grabbed his sheet and pillow from off his bunk.

As soon as Real was about to step out of the cell, J-Boy removed the covers from over his head, and sat up.
"Damn my nigga, you leaving without showing ya boy some love?"

Real was so excited about finally leaving he forgot all about J-Boy.

"Oh shit! Nah, it ain't even like that. I was just moving too fast that's all."
"I can dig it. When you get out there man just fall back and take care of ya family. You don't need to catch another case while you out on bail."

"I already know my nigga. I'm about to be out though, you got my cell number, call me if you need anything."

Real slapped hands with J-Boy before he rushed out of the cell and made his way to the CO's desk.

"Your escort is on their way now", the CO stated as he took Real's picture card out of a book and handed it to him.

The escort finally came to walk Real off the premises. When Real walked through the exit door and into the parking lot, he saw Tee Tee's BMW parked near the guard booth. *Damn man. Now how the hell am I going to get rid of her?* Real thought to himself in frustration.

Real continued to walk towards the vehicle. Being that it was his first day home, he knew it would be almost impossible to slip away from Tee Tee. All he wanted to do is go spend time with Nyla and his newborn son.

Tee Tee's eyes grew wide when she saw Real approaching the car.

"Oh shit! There go my baby! Baby, I missed you so much!" She exclaimed excitedly as she quickly climbed out to give him a big hug.

Real had only been locked up for two months, but to Tee Tee it felt like forever.

"I miss you too, babes. How you know I was getting out this morning?"

"When I went to go holla at Young A he told me that he just posted ya bail, and you would be out by the morning."

"Oh yeah? Did he say what was the hold up?"

"Nope."

Tee Tee noticed the disturbed look on Real's face.

"What's wrong?"

A fake smile slowly appeared on Real's face.

"Ain't nothing wrong babes, I'm good", Real lied, knowing damn well he was mad as hell she came to pick him up. "Take me to the

hood real quick, I need to check up on something."

Tee Tee snapped her teeth, putting her hand on her hip shifting all her weight to the opposite side.
"Nigga you ain't even been home five minutes yet, and you talking 'bout take you to the hood!"
"Calm down, I ain't even gon' be five minutes", Real said smoothly.

Tee Tee squinted her eyes at Real.
"You on the clock nigga, come on."

They both got in the car and pulled out of the parking lot.

Tee Tee drove through Real's neighborhood while he surveyed the area thoroughly, searching for Young A. *Where the fuck this nigga at?* Real said to himself in frustration. He grabbed Tee Tee's phone and looked at the time. It read 9:30AM, which was Young A's shift, so he definitely knew he was around somewhere.

"Park right here", Real commanded pointing at the deli on the corner.

Tee Tee parked in front of the deli like she was told.
"Don't be taking all long neither."

Tee Tee sat back in the seat and folded her arms across her chest. Real climbed out of the car. Young A was about a half a block away, on the side of an abandoned building serving one of Real's most loyal fiends.

"Come on Young A, you know I'm good peoples. You can give me a little bit more than that. I'm spending $40 dollars with you, not $25. It seem like ever since Real been gone I've been begging to get served the right way around here", the fiend complained as he held his hand out waiting for Young A to drop more crack in his palm. "Matter fact, when do Real get out?"

"He'll be out today", Young A replied as he took some more product out of a plastic bag and dropped it into the fiend's hand.

After that, the fiend cut through the back of the abandoned building which led to an alley way. Young A tied his plastic bag into a knot and stuffed it back inside his thermal pants before coming out of the cut.

Young A began walking down the street but quickly stopped in his tracks.
"Oh shit! I know that ain't my nigga."

Young A looked down the street and saw Real getting out of Tee Tee's car.
"Real!" he yelled out loud, walking towards him.

They were a nice distance away, so Real didn't hear him and kept walking. When Young A saw Real turn down the side street, he knew he was about to walk through the alley way so he quickly cut through the side of a house to meet up with him.

Real was walking through the alley way when he spotted Young A hopping the fence. *There that nigga go right there*, Real thought to himself. He started walking faster.

Young A was standing in the middle of the alley with a smile on his face when Real approached him.
"What's good bruh! I know it felt good as hell to finally be out of that shit hole."

When Young A tried to slap hands with Real, a hard-ass right-hook smashed against his jaw sending him stumbling back! Young A struggled to keep his balance.

"Nigga I missed my son come into this world because of you!" Real growled.

Real rushed towards Young A with the speed and force of a raging bull. Reacting off of adrenaline and natural reflex, Young A quickly grabbed his all black .38 snub nose from out of his front hoodie pocket and shot Real in the chest. BLOW!

Young A felt a twinge of regret as he watched Real stumble back and fall to the ground. His eyes were open wide as he stared down at Real who lay in the middle of the alley coughing up blood while holding the bloody hole in his chest.

Oh shit! Man what the hell did I just do? I know Tee Tee saw me cut through the side of the house! I know she knew he was coming out here to holla at me! Young A thought to himself panicking. His eyes scanned the alley way, hoping no one witnessed what just happened. He turned to look behind him and saw the fiend he just finished serving near the end of the alley staring directly at him. The fiend saw that Young A noticed him and took off running full speed out of the alley way.

"Damn!" Young A exclaimed, knowing that the fiend was too far away to catch up to him. He aimed his gun in the air and let off five rounds into the dark gray clouds. He then ran out of the alley way towards the deli. Tee Tee was bobbing her head to Monica's R&B lyrics bumping through her speakers. She noticed

Young A running towards her car. The music was so loud she didn't even hear the shots ring out.

"Call the ambulance! Call the ambulance!" Young A repeated as he approached the passenger car door. Tee Tee could tell by Young A's facial expression that something was wrong, but couldn't hear exactly what he was saying. She turned the volume down.
"What you say A?"
"Call the ambulance, hurry up! Them bitch ass niggas just shot Real! They just shot my bruh!"

Tee Tee gasped as she felt her chest tighten up. She quickly grabbed her phone from the passenger seat and called 911. While Tee Tee was on the phone, Young A tossed his gun in the sewer and climbed inside the car with her.

Tee Tee hung up with the dispatcher and turned to Young A. "They on the way!"
"Hurry up and drive through the alley!" Young A demanded.

When Tee Tee pulled up and saw Real lying in a pool of blood, she lost it!
"Oh my gosh, my baby!" Tee Tee cried hysterically.

She put the car in park and hopped out. She dropped down to her knees next to Real.
"Please baby don't die! Please don't die!" Tee Tee cried as she lowered her body to hug on Real, getting the warm blood all over her.

The ambulance finally pulled up and two paramedics jumped out the back with a stretcher. They scooped Real's body up, put him inside, and zoomed off.

CHAPTER 2

Nyla sat up in the hospital bed with baby Real cuffed in her arm feeding him a bottle of formula milk. It was no longer just her mother and daughter there to keep her company, a few other family members were there also. Everyone was celebrating the new life that just came into the world. They were all telling jokes, laughing, taking pictures, and reminiscing about the good ole days.

"I hope my nephew don't grow up to be anything like his grandpa on his dad side", Nyla's uncle Bill said looking at Nyla.

He sat in the chair next to her bedside. Uncle Bill was an old school slick-talking gangster that still did his thing in the streets every now and then.
"Why you say that, Uncle Bill?" Nyla asked.
"Because he was a cold-blooded sucker. I used to chase that joker from school all the way up to the 8th grade, but I never could catch him!"

Everyone in the room burst into laughter. "One thing my son ain't going to be is no sucker", Nyla adamantly protested. She looked on the table a few feet away, and noticed that the green light on her phone was clicking on and off.

"Tadasia hurry up and answer my phone, it might be Real calling", Nyla stated.

Tadasia hurriedly got up from her seat, grabbed her mother's phone and brought it over to Nyla. Nyla's hands were occupied, so Tadasia held the phone up to her ear.
"Run ya mouth", Nyla said.
"Nyla are you alright? This Janet."

Janet was her next door neighbor.

"Oh my fault girl, I thought you were my baby dad." "That's what I'm calling you about!" Janet said.

A perplexed look appeared on Nyla's face.

"Nyla I don't know how to say this, but, um..., Real got shot and it ain't looking too good for him."

"Real got shot!?" Nyla repeated in disbelief.

Everyone in the room immediately got quiet and looked at Nyla with concern.

"I hate to say it but I got my information straight from the news reporter on Channel Six News! It's still on, hurry up and try to catch it", Janet told her.

"Somebody hurry up and turn to Channel Six News!" Nyla shouted.

Her Aunt Tasha, who was already standing up, went over to the television and turned to Channel Six. Nyla's heart started beating rapidly when she saw Real's face on the television.

"Dan Duncan reporting live from the six hundred block of Martin Luther King Boulevard in Trenton. Not too long ago, a man identified as Real Johnson, a Trenton resident, was found in the alley way bleeding profusely from a gunshot wound to the chest,

and was rushed to Helene Fuld Hospital where he's now receiving treatment and is in grave condition. Detectives have no leads or suspects. Stay tuned for further updates..."

Just that fast they went from having a wonderful time celebrating the new life, to the tragic moment of possibly losing the man who helped create it. Everyone in the hospital room was completely silent. Some sadly shook their heads, some sighed deeply, but all of them stared at Nyla waiting for her reaction.

Nyla took the bottle out of baby Real's mouth and placed it on her lap. The tears began to trickle down her soft cocoa brown cheeks. "Can someone go find out what room he's in? I need to know he's okay!"

Uncle Bill got up from his seat and rushed out the room. His two sons, Johnny and Jeffrey, followed behind him. Nyla felt devastated, baffled, and extremely angry all at the same time.

Who the hell shot my baby dad? Why didn't he come straight here after he got out? I guess the boulevard was more important than being here for your newborn son, Nyla thought to herself as she looked in to Real Jr.'s innocent eyes.

The tears finally trickled off her face, falling on to Real Jr.'s blanket. Candace got up from her seat to console her daughter. "Nyla calm down baby, don't stress. We want your body and mind to heal properly after having this baby! Real is a very strong man. Have faith that he will be okay."

The silence that consumed the room was abruptly interrupted by the loud cries of Real Jr. Nyla only knew to grab the bottle of milk to try and feed him. He refused, and the cries became louder and louder. The frustration was evident, and after much straining the baby began to do a dry cough. Nyla leaned towards her baby's face. Beads of sweat mixed in with her tears. "Oh my God! Mom he is burning up!"

Candace felt her grandson's head. "We have to call the doctor in here." Candace pressed the button for the nurse's station, and pointed for a family member to go and find someone. The nurses and other family members rushed into the room within seconds.

"What's the matter?" The nurse was calm but her voice was strong and reassuring. They all rushed over to Nyla where the newborn was struggling to breath. "He won't stop screaming and his head is scorching hot!"

Nyla handed her baby over to the nurse.

"Go get the doctor!" The nurse demanded to her colleague. In the meantime, she took the baby's temperature. "He's at 103! We have to get this temperature down, honey. I don't want you to get too upset but this is critical. Pray and do all you know how to do in order to help us do what we have to do."

The doctor finally made it to the room and immediately began to assess Real Jr. "We have

to take him out, we will send for you shortly",
he said with authority.

Six or seven nurses moved in quickly,
working to get the baby cooler. They put cool
clothes in each of his hands and on his neck
and started an IV, then rolled the baby out of
the room. Nyla buried her face in her hands
and began to cry her heart out.

****

In the ER, Young A stood right beside Real's
bed side while Tee Tee sat in a chair next to
the bed. She held on to his hand with a tight
yet gentle grasp. Her deep cries and loud
sniffles played on Young A's conscious,
causing him to feel worse. Young A dropped
the first tear he shed in a long time. He shot
his best friend. The guilt was too much to
bear. *Damn Real*, he contemplated his fatal
decision.

Different tubes ran in and out of Real's body.
He lay in the hospital bed fighting for his life.
All of a sudden the room door swung open. It

was Uncle Bill and his two sons rushing though the door pulling back the curtain.

"How's he doing?" Uncle Billed asked.

"The doc said the bullet penetrated his chest 2 cm from his heart, and it ain't looking good", Young A informed the room.

Uncle Bill slowly walked towards Real, examining the condition. A somber feeling rushed over him as he reminisced on when he first met Real.

Back in the day Uncle Bill used to watch Real whenever he came to visit his niece, and he saw something in him. As the months passed by, he got to know Real personally and took a liking to him. Before you knew it, Uncle Bill had put him under his wing, and schooled him to the game. The rest was history.

"What the hell happened?" Uncle Bill looked to Young A for the answer.

Uncle Bill was smart. He had already felt the vibe of the energy in the room and was suspicious when he noticed that Young A was

avoiding eye contact. He stared at Young A, squinting his eyes as he waited for his response.

"Two niggas masked up came out of no where while we was in the alley way talking. These kids just started squeezing. By the time I got low, pulled my strap out, and started busting back, Real was hit! Don't even trip though Big Unc, I think I know who it is."

Even though Young A was lying straight though his teeth, he still sounded convincing. Uncle Bill slowly nodded his head.
"Oh yeah? You do huh?"

Uncle Bill had too much experience in the streets and knew something funny was going on.

"You know Real just bailed out from an attempted murder charge, right?" Young A emphasized, attempting to insinuate a new angle to keep the focus off him.

Uncle Bill nodded his head, knowing exactly what Young A was trying to say.

"Well it ain't nothing to talk about. You know what to do", he uttered making direct eye contact with the antsy young man.

"Yeah, you already know Big Unc, I'm on it!" Young A stated, but his eyes were not matching Uncle Bill's gaze.

"Well let me hurry up and get back upstairs to my niece so I can let her know her baby's father's status. You know she had Real's baby boy last night right?"

"Nah, Big Unc, I ain't even know that."

This time Young A glanced at Tee Tee as he lied.

Tee Tee began to feel all kinds of emotions flowing through her body. She actually thought she was the only one that Real was dealing with. She truly loved him. *How could he deceive me? Another female that probably ain't nowhere near my level just gave birth to his child last night?* Tee Tee thought to herself.

She released her grasp from Real's hand and wiped the tears from her beautiful face. It seemed like the more she wiped, the more tears poured from her watery eyes. She looked up at Young A and immediately felt betrayed knowing that he knew about Real's baby's mother. Tee Tee turned from embarrassed to angry and stormed out of the room.

Uncle Bill's eyes followed the young lady as she walked out. Then he looked at Young A with a raised eyebrow. "Who the hell was that?" He was so focused on Real and what Young A had been saying, he didn't take notice that she was in the room.

"Oh, that's my peoples, hold on real quick." Young A darted after her, dipping and dodging through the nurses in the hallway. When he finally caught up with her, she was stepping towards the exit door. "Tee Tee!"

The upset young lady just ignored him and kept walking. Young A understood why she was mad, so he didn't get angry and he

continued to follow her. He followed her through the exit door and jogged a few steps in front of her, stopping in time to turn and face her. Tee Tee stopped in her tracks and folded her arms across her chest.

"What do you want?!"

"I just wanted to make sure you..."

Before Young A could finish his sentence, Tee Tee interrupted. "I don't feel like talking right now. I just want to go home, take a shower, and get some rest. So where you want me to drop you off at?"

Young A just stood there trying to think of something to say to comfort her, but couldn't.

"Take me to my car, it's parked on the boulevard across the street from the laundromat."

"Aight, come on."

They walked together through the hospital parking lot, climbed inside of Tee Tee's BMW and pulled off.

****

38

"What the hell you mean my baby has to have surgery?!" Nyla asked raising her voice in the quiet hospital room. She was looking at the doctor like he had lost his mind. Uncle Bill had already told her about Real's unfortunate condition. The doctor inhaled and exhaled deeply feeling empathy for the young mother.

"It's like I've already said Miss McCoy, the formula is not agreeing with him. It has disturbed his immune system and made him very sickly", the doctor hesitated. "There's a strong possibility he might not make it through the surgery."

It was already bad enough that her babyfather was fighting for his life, now to hear that her innocent newborn baby was facing the same fate made it feel like her world was coming to an end.

The family was devastated. Nyla let out a loud cry. The stress of it all had her pulling on her long black silky hair. "I'm going to sue the shit out of this stupid ass hospital. You

muthafuckas gave my baby that milk! Fuck that! I need to see my baby and my baby dad!"

Nyla went to get out of her bed, but her Aunt Tasha, her mother Candace, and Uncle Bill restrained her. "Nyla calm ya nerves and lay down", Aunt Tasha demanded.
"You can't get out of the bed just yet, you have to let your body heal", Candace added while holding Nyla's lower body still.

The other family members Johnny, Jeffery, and Aunt Tasha's daughter Tiona watched with wide eyes as Nyla tried to break loose.
"Alright! Alright! Let me go!" Nyla cried.
She laid back down in the bed crying her eyes out in frustration. So many thoughts cluttered her mind at one time. It felt like her head was about to explode.
"You have to wait three more days before you'll be able to get out of this bed", the doctor told her.
"Fuck you!" she screamed.

Nyla reached over to grab the hospital phone from off the table and threw it at the doctor as hard as she could. The doctor quickly dipped to the side causing the phone to smash against the wall where it broke in to pieces. The doctor darted out of the room.

Candace looked at Nyla slowly shaking her head as she began caressing Nyla's hair to calm her.

"Don't drive yourself crazy, baby. Now is the time to pray and let God work his powerful miracles, you hear me?"

Nyla nodded while sniffling.

"Me and the family are about to go check on Real and the baby. We'll be back as soon as the surgery is over", Candace promised.

Little did they know, the unpredictable moment of life or death was just a few minutes away.

All of the McCoy women in the common room were summoned to the Neonatal ICU by a nurse who was extremely sympathetic. They stood over Real Jr. as he lay in an incubator. Candace looked down at her grandson, and

immediately felt weak in the knees. Seeing her grandchild hooked up to a respirator with those thick tubes running in and out of his tiny little frail body took a toll on her. It took everything inside of her to hold back the loud cries that burned the middle of her throat.

"Come on baby, make it through this for grandma and your family. You got to fight!" She said desperately holding baby Real's tiny little hand with her thumb and index finger. Baby Real wasn't even alive a full day yet and was already staring death in the eye.

At the same time, the men of the family were at Big Real's bed side. The sound of the breathing machines made a rhythmic sorrowful sound. Uncle Bill stood over Real Sr. with his arms folded across his chest. Uncle Bill then bent down so close to him that his lips touched his ear.

"Listen Real, I know you can hear me talking. This ya Uncle Bill. You going to fight your way through this like the soldier you are! And we..."

Before Uncle Bill could finish his sentence, the sound of the machines changed, the curtain opened and a swarm of doctors and nurses entered the room pushing and shoving everyone out.

Back in the NICU, the nurses and doctors wore white protective clothing and blue gloves, with masks that covered their mouths and noses.
"We need everyone to exit the room. It's time", one of the doctors announced.
Candace turned to face the doctor and asked, "How long do y'all think the surgery is going to be?"
"About forty-five minutes."
"Alright, thank you doctor."

Everyone was standing around crowding up the hallway when Candace finally stepped out of the room. She felt like breaking down but she told herself that she had to stay strong and keep everyone's spirits high.
"I don't know why everyone is just standing around. Y'all know what time it is. Form a

circle and grab each other's hand", Candace instructed.

Everyone formed a circle, grabbed each other's hand, and closed their eyes. They had the hallway blocked off, and Candace trusted no matter what those doctors did or said, God was the one who made the final decision when it came to baby Real and his father's fate. If anything the doctors were just his workers, there to do whatever He wanted done.

Candace started to pray as the tears rolled down her face.

"Dear Lord, you are the greatest Lord! You are the most powerful and I believe and have faith that you will snatch my grandchild and his father from the devil's treacherous grasp! We are well aware that this is one of his deceitful tricks to try and break this strong family down, but we refuse to let it happen Lord!"

Candace continued praying out loud while everyone prayed silently, letting the voice inside their hearts talk to God.

Everyone was so deep in prayer that it didn't seem like that much time had passed. The family didn't even hear the doctor walk up. At first the doctor didn't want to disturb them, so he stood there and waited for a little while. After about 2 minutes the doctor grew impatient and decided to clear his throat to get everyone's attention.

Candace's eyes popped open and she turned her head to see the doctor standing a few feet away.
"Amen", she whispered.
She released her grasp from the two hands she was holding and approached the doctor. Candace could tell by the look on his face that things didn't go well with the surgery.

The doctor took a deep breath and ran his hand across the top of his head.
"I have some good news and some bad news", he said sadly.
Candace swallowed hard, preparing for the news. "The good news is that the baby made

it through the surgery, but has developed symptoms of asthma in the process."

A wide smile slowly spread across Candace's face as she turned her head and looked back at her family smiling. They were all smiling and cheerfully hugging each other, thanking God for answering their prayers. She looked back at the doctor.

"The bad news is that we lost the child's father", the doctor told her.

Candace's smile quickly disappeared. She sighed deeply as she looked down at the white shiny floor. *Oh my goodness, Nyla is going to loose it,* she thought. Candace hated the stress that big Real put on her daughter by running the streets and creeping around with different women, but she still loved him and felt very bad about his death. Candace turned around and looked into Uncle Bill's sad eyes.

CHAPTER 3

Several days had passed. The pastor stood behind the podium with his face buried in the Holy Bible reading Psalms 81-83. Many attended the funeral to pay their respect to one of the realist to ever walk the streets of Trenton, New Jersey. Real laid peacefully in his silver plated casket. His makeup job was flawless, accentuating all of his best features. His hair was edged up just right, and his all white Versace suit made his chocolate skin appear as if it was glowing.

Nyla's loud sobs echoing through the church made the sad day even sadder. She leaned over the casket holding on to big Real's lifeless body as if she was about to try and pull him out.
"God why?! Why are you doing this to me?" Nyla cried.
Seeing the love of her life lying dead stiff in a casket was just too much for her to bear. She was slowly slipping away from herself. Her weight loss after delivering Real Jr. and the heavy bags under her puffy red eyes was an

indication that Nyla hadn't eaten or slept well since her mother told her the terrible news.

Candace, Uncle Bill, Aunt Tasha, and a few other family members sat in the front pew a few steps away from big Real's casket. Candace held baby Real in her arms. She could do nothing but shake her head at the sight of her daughter acting as if she had lost her mind. She knew Nyla was going to take it hard once she saw his body laid out, but not to this extent.

"Somebody grab Nyla and calm her ass down!" Candace demanded as she rocked baby Real back and forth in her arms.

Uncle Bill got up from his seat and stepped towards Nyla. She was still holding on to big Real crying her heart out when Uncle Bill wrapped his strong arms around her from behind. Nyla tried to break loose from his grasp but her resistance was in vain, Uncle Bill's hold on her was too tight.
"Get off me. Let me the go!" Nyla screamed.

"Nyla calm down this ya Uncle Bill. Calm down and have a seat", he whispered in her ear.

Nyla realized breaking loose from her uncle's grasp was not going to happen so she turned around, rested her head on his chest and began grieving even harder. "Everything is going to be alright baby girl. Your family is here for you", Uncle Bill stated, trying to comfort his niece as he gently rubbed her back.

Young A sat three rows behind the front pew. He wore an all black suit with black shades. His heart felt like it was slowly decaying inside of his chest as he observed Nyla mourning dramatically over his best friend's death. As bad as he wanted to get up from his seat and rush to Nyla's aid to console her, he just couldn't pull himself to do it. A tear slowly crept from underneath his black shades, and trickled down his cheek. He looked over at Tee Tee wearing an all blue dress. She was distraught and disgusted all in one twist and decided right then and there

that she was going to leave Trenton and never come back.

Crying uncontrollably, Tee Tee rose from her seat and stormed out of the exit door. Nyla and everyone in her family watched in wonder as she left out the church.

******

Later that night, Young A sat on the all black leather sofa in the living room of his one-bedroom apartment. He had on nothing but a pair of blue boxers. All of the lights were turned off and the only dim piece of light that beamed throughout the apartment came from the TV screen which sat on the wooden table in front of him. He watched the documentary of Rich Porter, crying uncontrollably as he held a fifth of Hennessy tightly in his hand. Young A didn't even drink, but being that it was going to be his last time breathing air on God's green earth, he said *fuck it why not*. He couldn't live with himself after killing his best friend and watching his family suffer.

Suddenly, he felt a very sharp pain in his stomach. Drinking all that liquor on an empty stomach caught up with him. He quickly leaned forward to spread his legs and began vomiting on the floor. Young A eventually sat back up, wiping the vomit from the side of his mouth. He threw the bottle against the wall with all his might but instead of it bursting, the bottle just bounced to the floor.

He dug his hand inside the couch cushions and pulled out a chrome 44 Magnum. He began shaking uncontrollably as he rested the barrel of the gun on the side of his head. Slowly placing his finger on the trigger, he cried out, "Please God, forgive me, for I have sinned!" Young A squeezed the trigger. "Aahh!"

Young A quickly jumped up out of a deep sleep. His whole body was drenched with cold sweat and he struggled to control his heavy breathing.
"Oh shit. It was just a dream", he said to himself out loud full of relief. "Thank God it was just a dream."

CHAPTER 4

Twelve years later, Real Jr. sat on the couch in the living room of his mother's run-down house waiting desperately for her to walk through the door. It's been two whole days since he last seen her. Although this wasn't anything new, Real began to grow worried. He knew that his mother loved him, but it seemed as if she loved the heroin habit she picked up after his father's death a little more. From time to time, when he used to go over his aunt's and uncle's house, he would hear his older cousins talking about how his mother use to be on top of her game until his father's death. After that, it was like Nyla had died and some weak minded, depressed heroin addict came alive.

Real Jr.'s family spoke a great deal about his father too. Real used to get angry when he overheard all the great things about him because he could only imagine what his father was really like, and how things would be if he were still alive. He could only imagine what

his mother used to be like and how things would be if she wasn't strung out on dope.

A hunger pain danced around in Real's stomach that was so sharp it made his eyes water. Real placed his hand on the side of his stomach, got up from the couch, and darted into the kitchen. That is where Real slept at night, on the floor in front of the stove with the oven door open and the heat on full blast. Everywhere else in the house was too cold due to the electric bill not being paid in months, so unfortunately the kitchen was his bedroom.

As soon as Real opened the refrigerator door the light came on and roaches began to scatter all over the rotten food and fruit that was inside. A foul odor assaulted Real's nostrils, causing his face to frown up. Real felt like he was about to die from starvation. He had to find some food and find it fast. He slammed the refrigerator door shut and then darted out the front door.

Real strolled through the entrance sliding glass doors of the neighborhood mini supermarket. This daily practice was nothing new to him. He already knew exactly what he had to do, where he was going, and what he wanted. His eyes scanned all over the store as he maneuvered through the crowds of people that were walking around grocery shopping.

Real reached his destination, the middle of aisle three where all the snacks were. He stopped and looked down both ends of the aisle and began grabbing a variety of cakes and cookies from off the shelves, stuffing them inside his sleeves and pockets. Out of nowhere, Real felt someone forcefully grab him by the hood of his snorkel coat. He jumped and quickly looked behind him with wide eyes and saw a tall white male security guard dressed in plain clothes. His heart began beating rapidly.

"What in the hell do you think you're doing?!" The security guard yelled looking down into Real's eyes.

Everyone in the aisle turned their heads to watch. Real tried his best to break loose and run off, but the security guard's grip was too strong.

"Get off me!" Real shouted.

"You're coming with me!"

Still holding on to Real's hood, the security guard swiftly wrapped his other arm around Real's waist, scooping him up, and carrying him towards the back of the supermarket where the supervisor's office was. Some of the onlookers shook their heads in disgust. "Let me the fuck go!" Real persisted.

The supervisor was seated at his desk looking over some bills he had just received in the mail, when the security guard busted through the door.

"We caught another one", the security guard smiled proudly.

He released Real from his grasp, closed the door and locked it.

"Now go have a seat at the desk and empty all your pockets", he ordered as he folded his arms across his chest. He posted up by the door just in case Real tried to run out.

Real felt ashamed and walked over to the desk with his head down. He sat in the chair in front of the desk.

The supervisor stared at him shaking his head as Real began pulling snacks from his pockets and placing them on the desk.

"So little man, please tell me what made you come here today and try to steal out of my store", the supervisor asked.

Real still had his head down, and remained silent for a few seconds. He finally responded in a low tone. "Because I was hungry. I ain't eat in almost two days."

"You mean to tell me, you didn't eat anything in two days?" he asked in disbelief.

Real nodded his head. "Um hum."

The supervisor looked at the security guard, and then back at Real.

"Where are your parents?"
"My daddy was murdered and I ain't see my mom in two days."

The supervisor began analyzing Real's attire and started feeling sorry for the poor kid. His snorkel looked as if it been through three of the most drastic blizzards Trenton had ever seen. Black duct tape covered the holes that were all over the sleeves. The zipper was broken, the right pocket was ripped halfway, and it barely had any lining inside. He had a pair of Jordan's on his feet that were entirely too small. It looked like his feet were about to bust out of the front at any given second. The sole was gone, visibly showing the wear and tear on the sneakers.

"Listen kid, I'm not going to call the police. You can have everything that you tried to steal out of my store today. But you have to promise that if you're ever hungry you will come here and let me know, instead of stealing from me!" The supervisor told him looking him directly in the eyes. A feeling of relief rushed over Real.

"I promise."
"Well, what are you waiting for, go ahead and eat", he gladly offered.

The store manager definitely didn't have to say that twice! Real popped open his snacks back to back and began stuffing more than he could chew inside his mouth. Within a few minutes, Real had finished munching down on the last honey bun and was as full as a house. The supervisor opened the blue and white cooler on the side of his desk, grabbed a flavored water out of it, and placed it on the side of the desk where Real was seated.
"You're going to be needing this."
"Thank you!"

Real grabbed the flavored water, took the top off, and began guzzling.
"I know you have someone in your family that I can call to come pick you up, because if not I'm going to have to call DYFS", the supervisor told him.

Real removed the bottle from his mouth and placed it back on the desk. "I don't know my

grandmom's phone number but I know where she live."

"And where's that?"

"...832 Southard St, apartment 2B, Dolly Homes Projects."

The supervisor looked at the security guard but before he could get a chance to get any words out of his mouth the security guard was already shaking his head with a terrified look on his face.

"Oh hell no, I'm not stepping one foot inside those crazy ass projects! Fuck that, y'all don't pay me enough for that shit!" The guard protested.

The supervisor frowned his face sharply, rose from his seat, walked to the coat rack and snatched his all black Polo jacket. "I'll take him myself then", he said sounding annoyed as he put his jacket on. "Come on little man, we're out of here." The supervisor walked out of the door with Real following behind him.

All eyes were on them as they climbed out of the Cadillac truck and began walking through the apartment complex with Real leading the way. The supervisor felt his chest tighten and wanted to run back to his car when he saw the crowd of young men dressed in all black wearing black masks on their faces with Remy Martin bottles in their hands standing in front of the buildings. Some of the hustlers and gangsters were just as afraid as he was when they noticed the unfamiliar white man walking through their projects. The first thought that ran through their heads was *POLICE!*

When Real and the supervisor finally stepped inside his grandmother's building they stopped and looked up at the busted light on the ceiling, which gave the hallway a dark and spooky feel. As they walked up the stairwell, they were taken by surprise when they saw an older woman wearing a blue scarf around her head, sitting on the steps smoking crack out of a chicken bone. Once the pungent smell hit their nostrils, they quickly covered their noses with their hands.

Brushing pass the woman, Real banged on the door as hard as he could and within seconds, the door swung open. "Grandma!" Real shouted happily as he fell into her open arms.

Candace took him into her grasp and held him tightly. The bright and wide smile that spread across both of their faces was enough to bring a little light to the dim hallway.

Candace glanced at the white man standing beside her grandson. *Who the hell is this at my door with my grandson,* she asked herself. The supervisor didn't want to spoil the lovely moment, but he had to hurry up and get back to work. He cleared his throat aloud.

"Excuse me but um, I'm the supervisor from Super G's mini market. I um…I caught your grandson stealing out of my store. Instead of calling the cops, I decided to just give him a ride home. He told me he hasn't seen his mother in two days and he hasn't eaten in two days, so I fed him until he was full", he

explained, noticing the disturbed look on Candace's face.

Not only was she embarrassed, but she was also sick and tired of her daughter's bullshit. This was definitely something she had grown accustom to. Every time Nyla would start messing up, Real would come and live with her for a while.

Candace was on welfare and had a serious gambling habit, but she still managed to maintain and did what she had to do most of the time. *This is the last fucking straw!* Grandma K thought to herself angrily.
"Words can't express how much I appreciate what you've done..."

Before she could finish her sentence the supervisor interrupted.
"It's no problem, don't worry about it."
"Would you like to come in and have something to drink?" she offered.
"I wish I could, but I have to hurry up and get back to my office", he told her as he looked

down at Real. "Don't forget about your promise little man."

"I won't forget", Real said smiling.

The supervisor turned around and made his way down the dark stairwell. Real and his grandmother went inside the apartment.

CHAPTER 5

Young Real sluggishly sat up in his bed, stretched his arms and let out a loud yawn as the wonderful smell of his grandmother's early morning breakfast greeted his nose. It smelled like she was cooking his favorite too! Cheese grits, cheese eggs, strawberry pancakes, and beef sausages fried hard. Real anxiously slid out of his bed and darted into the kitchen.

"Hey sleepy head! It's about time you woke up", Tadasia greeted him with a smile exposing her dimples as Real stepped into the kitchen. Tadasia was wearing skintight blue jeans that complimented her voluptuous thighs with a red long sleeved sweater that matched her red and black Jordan's. She had grown to be intelligent, beautiful, classy, strong, and ghetto, which made her every true dope boy's dream lady.

Although Tadasia and her family were struggling like majority of the people that lived in the projects, she carried herself as if

she was a queen in the truest form. She rose from her seat, and stepped towards the stove where she made Real's plate. She placed Real's plate on the glass table directly across from where she sat.

Real didn't waste any time. He sat down at the table, grabbed a spoon, and began stuffing his face. "Where's Grandma", Real asked almost in a mumble with a mouth full of food.

Tadasia strolled to her chair and sat in it.

"Boy if you don't stop trying to talk with food in ya mouth. Grandma left with Miss May like two hours ago. I think they went to play Bingo. You lucky I came over here in time, because if not you would've been sitting in Bingo all day bored out of your mind." She smirked, knowing how much her little brother hated going to Bingo with his grandmother.

"So mommy really left you in the house again by yourself, huh?" She asked seriously, looking her little brother in the face.

Real nodded while chewing his food. Tadasia exhaled, gazed down at the floor for a few seconds, and slightly shook her head. *Mommy back out there messing around again,* she thought to herself depressingly, before looking back up at her little brother.

"School starts in a few more days. I'm going to buy you a few outfits, a jacket, and a pair of sneakers."

Real's face lit up like a light bulb as he placed his spoon on his plate, finally finishing his food. Real loved when his sister went shopping for him, personally picking out his clothes. She always bought him the latest name brand wear that hit the market. Tadasia always protected Real and provided for her little brother with whatever he wanted and needed. That's whenever God blessed her with the opportunity to do so. It had been that way ever since Real could remember. The bond that the two shared was unbreakable.

Tadasia got up from her seat, grabbed Real's plate, and walked to the sink, where she washed and then placed it in the dish drainer.

Suddenly, loud rings from the phone in the living room began echoing throughout the apartment. RING! RING! RING! Tadasia quickly grabbed the paper towels off the counter and darted in to the living room. "Hello."

"I'm Dr. Lee. I'm calling on behalf of Nyla McCoy. She used this as her emergency contact. Who am I speaking with please?"

"I'm her daughter it's fine, I'm an adult."

"Ms. McCoy has been admitted here at St. Francis Hospital. She had a heroin overdose."

Tadasia's eyes widened as she gasped and placed her hand over her mouth. Her heart began beating rapidly as she listened intently to the doctor explain her mother's condition. Hot tears began sliding down her chocolate cheeks as she rushed back into the kitchen.

"Hurry up and get dressed", Tadasia cried looking at Real as she grabbed her jacket from off the chair.

Real saw the look on his big sister's face and knew something was terribly wrong. Without

asking any questions, he quickly stood up from his seat and did what he was instructed to do.

After reaching the hospital, Real and Tadasia quickly found their mother's room. The door was cracked halfway open. Real followed Tadasia inside and gently closed the door behind him. The two of them approached their mother's bedside. Real's eyes scanned the respirator mask that covered her mouth and nose, along with the tubes that were plugged into her skinny pale body. A somber feeling came over him. He didn't know exactly what was wrong with his mother, but from the little bit of information that his sister gave him on their way to the hospital he knew it was because of her drug habit.

Tears began sliding down Real's dark brown cheeks as he reached his arm out and gently grabbed his mother's cold hand. He then turned his head to look up at his big sister who was crying uncontrollably. Tadasia tried her best to keep her composure, but seeing

her mother laid out in the hospital bed barely alive was too much to bear.

Tadasia stared at her mother while her mind flashed back to all the arguments they had. At this moment she regretted every single harsh word she ever said to her mother. A twinge of guilt pierced her aching heart. *Mom please don't die. We need you,* Tadasia thought sadly trying to keep hope alive.

"You're strong, you can make it", she said softly.

Suddenly, Nyla began moving her head as she slowly opened her eyes. She let out a dry painful moan. Tadasia's mouth fell open, she was in shock.
"Mom!"

Real was relieved, and quickly became emotional and overwhelmed with joy. He couldn't do anything but stand there and smile as tears continued to pour down his cheeks.

Nyla grunted as she pulled the oxygen mask off her face, feeling strong enough to breath on her own.

"Mom! Mom!" Tadasia said excitedly as she leaned down to hug her mother.

Nyla hugged her daughter and kissed her forehead. She began feeling guilty and embarrassed that her kids were witnessing her in this condition.
"I'm sorry", she said.
"Please leave that stuff alone", Tadasia responded dramatically.

Nyla looked to her side and saw her handsome son's face standing teary eyed. A swarm of emotions came over her.
"Come over here boy and give me a hug."

Real smiled joyfully as he dove into her embrace.
"Mom what happened", he asked sounding concerned and confused.

Suddenly the hospital door swung open causing everyone to quickly turn their head. It Candace walking through the door. Tadasia called her grandmother when she was on her way to the hospital, she began to wonder what was taking her so long.

Candace felt relieved once she saw that her daughter was alive and well. The entire drive, she thought she was going to see Nyla laying on her death bed. She sighed deeply as she approached her daughter's bedside. Candace stared at Nyla for a few seconds.
"You see how much your family loves you!"

Nyla nodded her head.

"No you don't! Because if you did you wouldn't choose to rip and run them goddamn streets and pump that poison inside of your body!" Candace said raising her voice.

Candace was thankful that her daughter was alive, but she felt it necessary to put her in her place for repeatedly putting herself and the kids through the nonsense.

"When are you going to stop Nyla? Huh? You almost lost your life. God gave you another chance for a reason", she said looking Nyla dead in her eyes.

While Candace spoke, Nyla absorbed what her mother was saying with a deep thoughtful look on her face. She knew her mother was right but didn't know how to respond so she remained silent and just listened.

"If you're not going to stop messing with that poison for your own sake at least do it for the love of your children", Candace said desperately, waving her hand towards Tadasia and Real.

Nyla looked at her children, who were standing beside their grandmother with dried up tear streams on their faces. Nyla immediately felt ashamed and embarrassed. She felt like she had been coming up short ever since her son Real was born, and she knew she owed him true motherly love.

Nyla hated the fact that her children were witnessing her in the state she was in, and told herself *never again*. Never again would she put herself, nor her family through this turmoil.

"Mom please leave them streets alone. We need you alive and at home. Please promise us that you're going to sign into a rehab and get yourself together", Tadasia begged desperately.

"I promise baby, I promise", Nyla said without giving it a second thought. Nyla managed a slight sincere smile and opened her arms as her daughter fell into her embrace. "I'm going to sign into a rehab as soon as I'm released from the hospital."

Nyla never had agreed to go to a rehab so this was really a big step. Looking at her family she knew it was time. Candace began tearing up as she witnessed the love being displayed between her daughter and granddaughter.

"We're going to help you find one, a real good one too", Tadasia said seriously.

As soon as Nyla let go of her daughter, Real dove into her arms and tightly hugged her as if he never wanted to let go.
"I love you mom."
"I love you too baby. I want you to be good while mommy go away you hear me?" Nyla responded with a smile before she kissed him on top of his forehead.

Real nodded his head while still wrapped up in his mother's arms.

The warm feeling of family love mixed with the gratefulness she felt towards God for allowing her to make it through caused tears to flow from Nyla's eyes. It took for Nyla to almost loose her life for her to realize that it was time to make a new start and create a better drug free life that would be best for herself and for her children. God works in mysterious ways, doesn't he?

CHAPTER 6

The sun shone brightly from the skies above, but the gusty wind was an indication that winter was finally on its way. For majority of the students who enjoyed all of the wonderful moments the beautiful summer months presented, this day had come too fast. For Real, however, the first day of school took entirely too long to come. Everyday felt like a week as he anxiously anticipated wearing the new outfits that his big sister bought him for school.

Real stood in front of the project entrance gate peering at the boisterous crowd of children that congested the massive school yard directly across the street. They were all waiting for the bell to ring so they could get the day started.

Even though it was Real's first day of school and he didn't know too many people in the area, he still didn't feel one bit of nervousness. Instead he beamed with the pride and confidence of a young leader that did and had

everything he wanted in life. It showed all in his swagger as he began walking across the street when the school bell rang. It wasn't just because of his freshly dipped attire that made Real feel so proud inside, but it was also the promise his mother had made about getting her life together. Of course he heard her say it plenty of times before, but what convinced him this time was that she really took the step to admit herself to a drug treatment program.

The 8th grade math teacher Mr. Hammond stood before his class going over basic math facts the children learned last year. Real sat at a desk in the back right side of the classroom barely paying attention to what was being taught. Instead he had his face buried in a 10th grade math book. He loved math and studied it all the time so he was really on a 10th grade level.

Something told Real to look up, he felt someone staring at him. When he did, he saw to his left a red headed redbone girl staring at him. The girl must have wanted Real to know she was staring because she did not look

away when he caught her. The young girl snapped her teeth.

"Boy what is you looking at?"

Some of the other classmates turned their heads to look. Real looked puzzled, but he quickly regained his composure noticing that all eyes were on him. *What I'm looking at? YOU the one that been staring at me the whole period!* Real smirked to himself.

"You know that's funny because I've been thinking the same exact thing for about 30 minutes now. But since you asked first", he paused for a few seconds looking dead in her green eyes, "I guess nothing."

The classmates began chuckling while she frowned. She finally rolled her eyes and turned around in her seat.

"Excuse me class, this is a place to learn, not to make jokes", Mr. Hammond announced firmly staring directly at Real who had quickly buried his face back in to his book.

This was the first day of school and Mr. Hammond knew that if he didn't put his foot down today the students' behavior would only get worse as the year went on.

"Mr. Johnson", Mr. Hammond said firmly to Real.

Once he saw that he had Real's full attention he continued.

"Since you've been paying attention more than everyone else in the class, I would like for you to come up here and answer this math problem for the class."

Mr. Hammond turned around to face the chalkboard and wrote down a problem he thought would be challenging for a new student to solve. Real slid out of his seat, looking at everyone boldly as he walked up to the front of the classroom. Mr. Hammond handed him the chalk and folded his arms across his chest.

Real looked at the problem on the chalkboard and wanted to burst out in laughter. *Come on*

now, you could've done better than that, he thought to himself. Real began writing on the chalkboard and within seconds the math problem was solved. He turned to look at Mr. Hammond and couldn't help but smirk when he noticed the surprised look on the teacher's face. *This clown tried to play me and got played,* Real said to himself.

Real handed the chalk back to the surprised math teacher and started clapping his hands together, dusting the residue off. He turned around to face the other students in the classroom.

"For now on, if anybody is trying to learn something about math, I'm the nigga you need to holla at!" Real announced arrogantly.

Suddenly, the bell rang letting everyone know the class was over. Everyone began grabbing their books and making their way out of the classroom. Mr. Hammond walked over to his desk near the exit door feeling a little defeated. *Who the fuck does this nappy-headed mother fucker think he is? This is my classroom! I run the show here!* Mr. Hammond thought to

himself angrily as his eyes watched Real walk proudly to his desk to grab his belongings.

"Aight Mr. Hammond, see you tomorrow. I appreciate the lesson you taught us today", Real said chuckling as he strolled passed the teacher's desk.

When Real entered the lively overcrowded cafeteria he found a spot in back of the long lunch line and patiently awaited his turn to come so he could grab his tray and have a seat. His eyes scanned the cafeteria in search for a perfect spot to sit. He noticed the red head girl from his math class staring at him again. *You just can't help it huh,* he said to himself as he smiled and nodded his head at her. She stuck her middle finger up at him, turned back towards her friends, and whispered something to them. They all peeked at Real and began giggling. *Joke's on me huh? Well I want to laugh too,* Real thought. He was no longer in search of a spot to sit, because as soon as he grabbed his lunch tray he was going over to where the girls were sitting to find out what was so funny.

When Real reached his hand out to grab his tray from the kitchen worker, a tall chubby kid with box braids in his hair rudely cut in front of him and snatched it from out his hand. He turned around and mean mugged Real.

"New niggas don't eat! So for now…"

Before the kid could finish his sentence, a right overhand crashed against his nose bone, cracking it. Blood instantly began leaking out like a faucet as the kid stumbled back falling flat on his face! He was knocked out cold! All the students screamed and yelled as they bum-rushed Real. He quickly turned around with his guard up. While he had his back turned and focused on the crowd, another kid with a low haircut crept up from the blind side and swung a wild blow that rocked Real's world. He stumbled into another kid that looked exactly like the one that caught him from the blind side! He grabbed Real from behind and tried to slam him on his head, but couldn't due to Real's resistance.

As the two struggled to gain control over one another, a dark skin kid with long tiny braids hanging down his back slid out of the rambunctious crowd of on-looking students, and swung a stiff uppercut that landed on the kidney of the kid tussling with Real. "Agghh!" he yelled in agony as he fell to the floor and curled up holding his side.

The dark skin kid began stomping him relentlessly! Real was able to regain his composure and rushed the other kid that punched him from the blind side. He swung a swift jab followed by a right hook, but the twin managed to dip both of the punches and grabbed Real by his shirt. The two began tussling all over the cafeteria before falling to the ground. The sound of metal folding chairs and lunch trays could be heard down the hall. Within seconds, a swarm of security guards came blitzing through the cafeteria.

"Move the fuck out of the way!" One of the security guards shouted as they pushed their way through the crowd of students who were circled around the wild brawl. Real and the

other twin still were wrestling on the floor trying to gain control. The gang of security guards moved in to restrain them and all the other participants involved in the brawl. Real tried his best to pull away from the security guard who was holding on tightly to the back of his shirt.

"Get the fuck off me. I can walk on my own."

Real glanced and briefly spotted the red head girl in the midst of the crowd looking directly at him.

The two security guards that escorted Real and his unexpected helper with the long braids to the principal's office introduced themselves as Terrence and Darrell. Terrence was tall, light skin with a bald head, while Darrell was short with brown skin and a low cut. Darrell held the principal's office door open and stared both of the boys down as they walked into the office.

"Have a seat and don't touch nothing!"

While Darrell and his partner Terrence began talking in the hallway, Real and the kid with

the long braids sat in two chairs a few feet across from each other and began surveying the principal's cluttered office. There were stacks of papers scattered all over the desk, with piles of cardboard boxes filled with books sitting on the floor near the window. The place was a complete mess. Real's jaw ached and his blood boiled inside his veins, but he still couldn't help but stare at the wild looking young boy that came to his aid with a look of wonder on his face.

The kid sat slumped in his seat with his arms folded across his chest looking at Real look at him.
"The name's Kaze my nigga. What's yours?"
"Real."

They both got up from their seats and slapped hands with each other before sitting back down.

"Good looking for the helping hand. Them bitch ass niggas was on my ass!" Real admitted.

"That shit ain't about nothing. I been beefing with the twins the whole summer!" Kaze told Real.

"Oh yeah?"

"Yeah. They always jump me because they can't beat me one on one! That's why when I saw you giving it to them niggas I jumped in. I would've been a fool not to, you feel me?"

Real nodded his head knowing that he would've done the same thing.

"Well whichever one of them hit me from the blind side gotta see me", Real said excitedly as he slammed his fist into the palm of his hand. Real wasn't just angry about getting punched from the blind side, he was also angry because the twin dipped his two piece and stretched his shirt. "And who the hell was that nigga? The…"

Before Real could finish his sentence he heard the door knob twisting, he quickly calmed down and shut his mouth. The door opened and the principal walked in. The principal

was a short white older man with a bald head, he wore a grey suit.

"Oh so these are the two little tough guys that started the riot in my cafeteria on the first day of school?"

The principal then sat down in the chair behind his desk and began searching through the scattered papers.

"I ain't start nothing, I finished it", Real stated boldly.

Kaze began chuckling. Darrell and Terrence stepped inside the office and posted up by the door side by side.

"Oh so you're not just a tough guy you're a smart ass too. I wonder what you're going to say to your mother when she finds out that you're suspended for 9 days because you started a riot!" The principal threatened.
"My mom ain't going to care when I tell her what happened so you just wasting your time and breath."

The principal grew furious. Two things he couldn't stand was when a student disregarded his authority, and when they challenged him verbally. Real was doing both, which made him lose it. Darrell and Terrence were completely shocked at how Real was talking to the principal.

"I think the new kid is going to be a big problem", Darrell said in a low tone looking at his partner.

"Yeah, me too", Terrence agreed.

"Oh your mom isn't going to care, huh?" The principal quickly hopped out of his seat and stormed towards Real. "That's going to be the same reason you end up dead or in jail for the rest of your life before you turn 18! Just like all the other kids that came through here with the same rotten attitude."

Real looked away as if he wasn't paying attention.

"Do you hear me you little piece of shit! You're going to be a fucking failure when you grow up!"

Breathing heavily, he stormed back over to his desk and sat down to sign the suspension papers.

"Here! Get this little disrespectful motherfucker out of my office!" The principle barked as he handed Darrell the suspension papers.

"Come on fellas, follow me through the hall", Darrell ordered as he handed Real and Kaze a copy of their suspension papers. Darrell and Terrence walked through the door of the principal's office. Real and Kaze stood up from their seats and followed them. They were taken to in-school detention where they spent the remainder of the day writing a 1,000 word essay on why they shouldn't start riots. The other kids that really started the brawl were in another detention class on the 3rd floor. They only received 5 days of in-school

detention because the kitchen worker said that Real threw the first punch.

The first day of school was finally over and crowds of students poured out of every exit door in the building. They were all eager to go home and tell their families how their first day of school went. Real and Kaze, on the other hand, felt the total opposite. The new friends walked slowly through the school yard while all the other kids were anxiously speed walking and running pass.

"Man, it felt like we was in that soggy ass detention class for two days", Real complained.

"Hell yeah! It felt like my hand was about to fall off writing that long ass essay!" Kaze replied.

"Man, as soon as I got to the third sentence I ran out of shit to say, so I started writing the same thing over and over again!"

Real looked at Kaze, waiting for his response. He noticed the dumbfounded look on Kaze's face and knew exactly what was wrong.

"Let me find out you was really in there busting your brain trying to complete that whack as essay!"

Real placed his hand on his stomach and burst into laughter. Feeling embarrassed, Kaze couldn't do anything but shake his head and chuckle.

"Oh shit, look. There go the twins right there", Kaze shouted pointing towards the corner deli across the street. Real quickly looked and saw the twins coming out of the store.

"Damn, where the nigga I knocked out at?" Real wondered.

"Shit! He probably still in the cafeteria sleep!" Kaze responded chuckling.

"Come on!" Real said taking off running.

Kaze followed him.

Real and Kaze finally caught up with the twins who were walking down a side street. They stopped running and began silently speed walking behind them. Real could tell the twins apart because the one Kaze stomped

out had bruises all over his face. The twins were deep in conversation and barely paying attention to their surroundings.

Kaze grabbed the one he stomped out by the jacket and swung him around violently, slamming his head against a parked black pickup truck, knocking him out instantly. As the other twin turned around to see who was behind him, a right hook came across his jaw, sending him stumbling back.

"I hope y'all ain't think that shit was over!" Real hollered as he put his guard up.

The twin caught his composure and rushed Real and swung a sloppy right hook. Real dipped low and countered with a short, stiff double hook to his rib cage.

"Agghh!" the twin groaned in agony as he grabbed his side and backed up, gasping for air.
"My sister can throw a punch better than that!" Real teased as he began bouncing around.

Kaze smiled at his new found friend's humor, and began clapping his hands together.

"You looking real good out there boy", he shouted between his laughs.

While Real was looking at Kaze, the twin charged him and threw a wild right hook. The hard blow landed on Real's jaw and sent him stumbling backwards. Real struggled to catch his balance, he tripped over a cinderblock that was in the middle of the sidewalk, causing his back to violently crash against the pavement. Kaze immediately stopped laughing.
"You aight my nigga?"

Kaze looked up at the twin Real was fighting, put his guard up, and began stepping towards him. He already had it in his mind that once the twin landed one punch he was jumping in.

"Fall back Kaze. I got him", Real ordered.
Kaze kept stepping towards the twin.

"Man them niggas ain't never let me get no straight up, fuck that!" Kaze growled without taking his eyes off the twin who was slowly backing up.

"Fall back my nigga, I got this! Trust me! The way I'm about to beat this nigga ass it's going to be like we jumped him", Real assured Kaze as he got up from the ground.

Kaze slowly put his guard down and stepped to the side to let Real handle his handle. A young hustler standing in the middle of a crowd down the street watched.

"Yeah Twin, beat that little nigga the fuck up!" He yelled.

Everyone standing on the corner quickly turned their heads and saw Real and the twin bouncing around on their toes, throwing punches at each other. They rushed towards them.

"I got two hundred on twin!" One yelled.

"I got three hundred on twin!" Another yelled

"I got five hundred on twin."

Several of the young men began placing bets and pulling money out of their pockets while crowding around Real and Twin. Everyone was cheering for Twin to win the fight because he was from the area, and no one had ever seen Real before. Then, out of nowhere, a brown skin young man with neatly twisted dreads and a tattoo of a hundred dollar bill on his neck stepped in the middle of the crowd.
"I got my money on the little dark skinned nigga!" he announced.

The brown skin man pulled out two wads of cash from his True Religion jean pockets and began placing bets with everyone in the crowd. Twin swung a double jab but Real dipped both of the punches. Hearing someone finally place a bet on his behalf gave Real the energy he needed.

While Real and the twin was getting it in, Kaze turned and saw the other twin slowly getting back up trying to regain his composure. Kaze quickly rushed towards him and swung a right hook with all his might

that landed on his chin knocking him back out cold.

Over on Real's side, the fight was live!
"Why you keep backing up. What you scared now nigga?"

Every time Real made an attempt to rush in, Twin swiftly backed away. He was trying to stick and move after feeling how hard Real's punches were.

A full minute passed by and the charged up crowd followed as Real backed Twin into the thick black project gate. Real faked a right, causing the twin to step into a stiff left double jab and a powerful leaping right hook that landed right on his chin. Everyone in the crowd gasped as Twin dropped down to one knee. He put his hand on the ground in order to prevent himself from falling. His eye was split and his mouth was busted wide open.
"Yeah, get back up! Come on!" Real taunted as he took a few steps back bouncing up and down with his guard still up.

The twin tried slowly getting up but with wobbly legs he staggered a little bit before falling flat on his face. Everyone who bet against Real stood silently with dumbfounded looks on their faces. The young man with the tattoo and dreads laughed uncontrollably while collecting his winnings from everyone.
"I knew that young boy was going to beat Twin's punk ass! All him and his brother good for is a jump!"

Real walked over and slapped hands with Kaze.

"I told you I had everything under control my nigga." "Yeah, you definitely did your thing", Kaze replied. "Aight, lets get out of here."

Real and Kaze began walking off, but the young man with the dreads approached them from behind with a blunt in his mouth, counting a wad of cash in his hand.
"A yo, young boy."

Real and Kaze both turned to face him at the same time.

"You walking away like you don't want no money", the young man said.

Real and Kaze just stood there staring at him without saying a word. The young man handed Real four crispy bills. Without looking at how much he had, Real hastily stuffed the cash into his pocket. "Thanks!"

The young man took a deep pull on the blunt and slowly blew the smoke out.

"It ain't no need to thank me. You earned that li'l bruh! With those quick hands, you supposed to be in the ring some where!" He laughed thinking about how Real just punished his opponent.

Kaze just stood there quiet the whole time as the two talked to each other.

"What's your name?" the young man asked.
"Real."
"You sure you can live up to that name?" The young man smirked.

"I was born with it so I guess I ain't got no choice."

The young man nodded his head. *I like this little nigga,* the man thought to himself.
"What's your name?" Real asked.
"I'm Benji, and I'm going to live up to my name until I'm laying in the dirt! You know how I'm going to do that?" He asked getting animated while looking Real in his eyes.

Without giving Real a chance to answer he continued.
"By getting this fucking paper. That's how." Benji tapped his hands on his two front pockets that were bulging with cash.

After that, it was all she wrote. Once Benji started talking about money and how to get it, he just couldn't stop. He loved touching that paper. That's what he lived for. He was addicted to the feeling that traveled through his body when it was time to go hard and get it.

Benji kept going on and on about himself and the hustle while Real and Kaze listened. Pure admiration was beaming from their eyes as they soaked everything up like sponges. After listening to Benji talk for almost an hour, Real and Kaze told him they would holler at him later, and they began walking towards the deli on the corner.

Loud Spanish music filled their ears as soon as they stepped inside the deli. The short, chubby Puerto Rican man who looked to be in his late 30's, stood behind the counter. He discretely reached his arm out wrapping his hand around a chrome .357 Magnum that rested on the side of the cash register. The young hustlers from the neighborhood protected the store from the stick-up boys in exchange for being able to sell and stash their product inside. This protection didn't stop Papi from staying on point and wishing someone would try to rob him so he could blow them away.

Real and Kaze grabbed everything they wanted and placed it on the counter.

"How much Papi?" Real asked pulling out the money Benji gave him.

His eyes grew as wide as two 50 cent pieces when he looked down at the four crispy hundred dollar bills in his hand.

"Oh shit, Benji must have slipped up and gave me the wrong bills", Real exclaimed as he showed Kaze the money.
"Yeah he probably did, you better hurry…"

Before Kaze could finish his sentence, Real rushed out of the deli and darted back up the street. Benji was just about to pull off in his blue 600 Benz blasting Young Jeezy through the speakers. Real ran up on the driver side door and tapped on the window.
"A yo, Benji!"

Startled a little, Benji turned his head and quickly grabbed hold to his chrome Colt 45 handgun that rested on his lap. Once he saw that it was Real, he eased up and smiled. Benji turned down his music and lowered the window.

"What's good little bruh? You aight?"
"I think you made a mistake and gave me the wrong bills", Real told him.

Real was trying to hand him the money through the window. Benji looked inside Real's hand and shook his head. He smirked knowing if that was any other young boy he would've just been beat for his money.

"Nah. I ain't make no mistake, lil bruh. That's all you right there. I appreciate the honesty though. Keep living up to your name. It'll get you a long way."

Benji turned the volume all the way up, leaned back in his seat, and pulled off. The Young Jeezy lyrics blared through the speakers. *"I command you niggas to get money! I command you niggas to get money!"*

After Real watched Benji pull off, he went back to the deli, paid for his items, and split the rest of the money with Kaze. The new friends continued to walk home. Once they

got near Real's grandmother's building reality began to sink in. *How the hell I'm going to tell grandma I got suspended on the first day of school?*, he thought to himself. Real pondered whether he should tell her or not. Kaze turned to look at Real as they walked side by side.

"Damn my nigga. What you about to do walk me to my door?" Kaze said jokingly trying to free Real from his thoughts.

"That's funny, because I was thinking the same thing.

I live right there!" Real said, pointing to his grandmother's building.

"Oh yeah? Thats what's up because I live in the building right across from yours on the 1st floor."

The mentioning of his grandmother made him think about the consequences of him getting suspended.

"A yo, Kaze, if I tell my grandma I got suspended on the first day of school she fuck around and put me on punishment for like two months!"

"Then don't let her know. All we got to do is get the suspension papers the school going to send before our peoples do and act like we going to school everyday."

Real thought about what Kaze said for a few seconds, and then nodded in agreement.

"Aight, say no more. That's what it is", Real said.
"Meet me in front of the deli in the morning", Kaze told him.

Real and Kaze slapped hands and went their separate ways into their buildings.

CHAPTER 7

The following days Real and Kaze did exactly what they had planned, they pretended to attend school without their parents taking notice. They both managed to sneak the mailbox key and intercept the suspension papers. Everything was going smoothly until the 9th day when they took the truancy officers on a wild foot pursuit and got caught. Kaze and Real were taken down to the board of education to provide their information, but the two slicksters gave false names. Once their pictures were taken they were released.

That was a close one, Real said to himself relieved. He opened the door and stepped inside his grandmother's apartment, letting the door slam shut behind him.

"Real, is that you baby?" Candace yelled from the kitchen. She was seated at the kitchen table talking on the phone.

"Yeah it's me grandma."

"How was school?"

"It was fun."

Real approached his grandmother, lowering his head and kissed her on the cheek causing her to smile.

"While I was out shopping earlier I grabbed you a few outfits and a pair of sneakers."

Real's face lit up like a Christmas tree.

"Where they at?" he asked anxiously.

Candace couldn't help but chuckle at her grandson's excitement. "They're in your room on the bed."

Real darted out of the kitchen and made his way to his room. As he approached his bed, he let out a deep sigh. There he saw the big white plastic bags with PAY-LESS written all over them. He dug in the bag and pulled out three ugly outfits and a brown box with sneakers inside. He opened the box and shook his head in disgust. It was a pair of green and white Eagle sneakers. He put the lid back on the box and put everything back inside of the bag. *If I wear this bullshit to school I'll be laughed*

at ten years from now. Hell no!!! Real thought heading back to the kitchen.

When he approached his grandmother, she was just hanging up the phone.
"Thanks grandma."
"You're welcome baby", Candace said smiling.

Real had a wide smile pretending to be happy as he leaned forward to hug Candace. If his mother didn't teach him anything else she taught him how to be thankful whenever someone gave him something, even if he didn't like it.

Candace grabbed her purse from off the glass table and got up from her seat.

"I'm about to go to Miss May's house and play cards. You know the number to her house if you need me", she said before putting on her jacket and rushing out the door.

As soon as Real heard the door shut and the lock turn, he grabbed the phone and dialed Kaze's number. "Hello", Kaze answered.

"What's good my nigga, this Real. Come to my crib, I gotta show you something", Real stated depressingly. "Aight, I'm on my way over there right now."

Five minutes hadn't even gone by, and Kaze was already knocking on the door. KNOCK! KNOCK! KOCK! Real was seated on the couch in the living room.

"Come in."

Kaze opened the door and stepped inside the apartment.

"What's up? What you got to show me?" Kaze asked eagerly.

"Come back here."

Real stood up from the couch and made his way to the back room. Kaze followed him. Real grabbed the plastic bags off his bed and handed them to Kaze who frowned when he noticed the PAY-LESS logo on the bag. Kaze began looking though everything inside the

bag. His struggles were no different from the majority of the kids in the ghetto, but he damn sure didn't have to wear PAY-LESS!

"Awe man, who got you this bullshit?" Kaze asked.

"My grandma, but I ain't wearing that whack shit to school! I rather wear the clothes my sister got me over and over again than wear that!"

"How many outfits she bought you?"

"Three."

"Nah my nigga, you ain't got to do yours like that. I got a couple of outfits you can wear."

Kaze started putting Real's clothes back in the bag. Usually Kaze would've made a joke of this, but this particular situation was way to embarrassing to laugh about. Real wanted to take the outfits from Kaze, but his pride wouldn't let him.

"That's good looking out but I'm good."

Kaze looked at Real like he was crazy.

"So you mean to tell me you rather were three outfits for the whole school year?"

"I guess so", Real responded in a low tone with a stupid look on his face.

"What you mean you guess so? Do you know how that's going to look? We fly gangsters, we can't come like that."

For the next 10 minutes Kaze tried to talk Real into wearing his clothes. Real finally got tired of hearing Kaze's mouth.

"Aight man, I'm going to wear them. Damn!"

Kaze smiled, knowing Real was going to give in eventually. "I don't know why you acting all crazy and shit. Let's go outside and get some fresh air."

Real and Kaze strolled through the black public housing exit gate that led onto the boulevard. They stopped in their tracks in complete awe as they surveyed the scenery with wide eyes. It looked as if someone was setting up for a video shoot. A variety of new model cars took up every parking spot on the street as loud music blared through almost

every car speaker, making it impossible to make out what songs were being played.

A crowd of young men and women were gathered around two separate dice games a few feet away from each other. They were all fresh to death with ice dripping from their necks, wrists, and ears.
"Damn!" Real exclaimed in amazement, turning to face Kaze. "It's live as hell out here today."

Kaze nodded his head in agreement. He was just as excited as Real.
"Yeah I know right!"

Real pointed towards one of the crowds while still looking at Kaze and said, "That's how we supposed to be."

Kaze glanced across the street, "Oh shit check Benji out."

Real quickly turned and saw Benji getting out of his Benz. His dreads were done neatly in French braids and he had more chains than

Mr. Tee wrapped around his neck. The solid gold charm with the initials M.O.E. imprinted inside of it flooded with the black diamonds and green emeralds stood out the most. He wore a black and green Gucci spring jacket with the Gucci shoes to match. After he glided across the street he began collecting money from the young men that were shooting dice and the ones that stood on the corner in front of the deli.

Real took his eyes off Benji and started looking around at everyone on the block. He noticed that they were all doing the same thing he and Kaze were doing, which was watching Benji. It was as if Benji had everyone on the block in a trance.

Real looked back at Benji and saw him climbing back into his Benz. Benji pulled off and beeped the horn at Real and Kaze as he drove pass. They both gave him a head nod, and watched him cruise down the boulevard. The way Benji just pulled up and had the block on pause only added to the admiration they already had for him. To them, Benji was

the flyest gangster in the world, and you couldn't tell Kaze and Real anything different!

"You saw how Benji hopped out the Benz swagged up with all that ice dripping?" Real said excitedly. "Hell yeah, that nigga looked like a movie star."

All of a sudden, the loud sound of tires screeching filled the air causing everyone on the block to quickly turn their heads. Unmarked cars and trucks were pulling up from all angles, slamming on their brakes, and running up on the crowd. Plain clothes officers jumped out of their vehicles and chased after a few of the young men that ran. The other officers made everyone else standing around get on the ground face down then began searching everyone.

Real and Kaze were watching them raid the premises when one of the detectives wearing a mask stormed their way.
"Take your little asses home before we throw cuffs on you too!" The detective barked.

"Fuck you! Come on Kaze!" Real yelled boldly.

The two friends ran back through the projects as fast as they could.

CHAPTER 8

Only two weeks had passed and Real was already fed up with wearing Kaze's clothes to school. He felt everyone who stared at him too long knew that he was wearing his best friend's clothes, which made him feel uncomfortable. Real locked his grandmother's door and started walking down the stairwell. Once he made it to the first floor he opened his book bag and pulled out an outfit Kaze let him borrow.

"This my last time doing this shit", Real mumbled.

He pushed the heavy hallway door open and went into Kaze's building, darting up the first flight of steps. Just as Real balled up his fist to knock on the door it swung open and Kaze came rushing out with his head turned not paying attention.

"Damn bruh slow down", Real said.

Kaze jumped as he turned to see Real standing in front of him.

"Oh shit! You was just about to knock on the door, wasn't you?" Kaze asked smiling.
"Yeah", Real said sounding depressed.

Real turned around and started walking down the stairway. Kaze stood still in the doorway for a few seconds, never taking his eyes off of Real. He could tell that something was bothering him.
"Whats good bruh? You aight?"

Kaze jogged up on the side of Real and began walking with him. Instead of responding right away, Real continued walking with his head down. He finally slowed down.
"Something got to give man. I can't keep going through this."

A look of confusion appeared on Kaze's face.
"Keep going through what?"

Real looked back down at the ground as he let out a deep breath, and then looked back up at Kaze.
"Being looked at funny and probably clowned because I'm wearing your clothes to school."

"Man nobody don't know you wearing…"
"Yes they do. I can tell by the way they look at me."

Real was right, almost everyone in the school knew that the clothes he wore were hand-me-downs from Kaze because all of the outfits were from Kaze's wardrobe the previous year.

"So like I said, I'm done with doing mine like this. As soon as school let out, I'm going to holla at Benji and tell him to put me on my feet so I can take care of myself." Real was dead serious.

Kaze and Real continued talking as they walked through the parking lot. Kaze thought about what Real just said and couldn't do anything but respect it. "You saw how fly them niggas was dressed the day them police raided? You saw all the jewelry they wore, stacks of money they held in their hands? Man, and how all them bad ass bitches stood around them like servants?"" Real said getting amped up and animated .
"Yeah", Kaze nodded.

"That's the life I want to live."

"Well if that's the way you want to live, lets live it then. I'm with you one hundred percent no matter what!"

Kaze noticed the smirk on Real's face.

"What's so funny?"

"Nothing my nigga, nothing", Real replied chuckling.

Real was so used to doing everything on his own that when he heard Kaze say that he was with him no matter what, an unfamiliar feeling of joy came over him.

A few hours had passed, and everyone in Mr. Hammond's classroom was in complete silence and was focusing in on their math test. Real completed his test 10 minutes early, so he was just sitting at his desk with his arms folded across his chest. His stomach growled like a vicious pit bull's. *Man I wish these five minutes hurry up and pass by, I'm hungry as hell*, Real thought while staring at the big white clock on the wall over top of Mr. Hammond's desk. Real turned and smirked when he

caught the red headed girl staring at him for the hundredth time.

Within minutes, class was finally over and everyone rushed out the door. Real walked hurriedly through the congested hallway with his math book in his hand. Several young boys that were posted up in the hallway acknowledged Real's presence with hand shakes and head nods as he walked passed them, heading towards his locker.

Ever since Real came back from his suspension he noticed how everyone was acting friendly towards him, but paid it no mind. Unbeknownst to him, word traveled throughout the school that the new kid had heart and no matter win, loose, or draw he wasn't taking no shorts.

Real placed his book inside of his locker and walked towards the cafeteria. Suddenly, he heard an unfamiliar female voice scream his name.
"Real!"

He stopped and turned around and saw a brown skin girl waving her hand, motioning for him to come to her. As he walked towards her she met him halfway. "What's good?" Real asked.

Her neatly French-braided hair hung down to the middle of her back.
"Hey Real my name's Qadeesha. My cousin Dynasty told me to ask you do you want to be her boyfriend."

Qadeesha noticed the puzzled look on Real's face and continued, "She's the red headed girl in your math class."
"I know you ain't talking about who I think you talking about", Real said with raised eye brows.
"Um hum, you're going to see her in the cafeteria this lunch period."

Qadeesha turned around to walk away but remembered something.

"Oh yeah, tell your friend Kaze I like him."

Qadeesha smiled and finally walked off. Real watched her disappear amongst the crowd of kids in the hallway. He turned around and noticed that Kaze was walking towards him. He shook his head, and thought, *right on time, wait until my boy hear this hot shit!*
"What's good bruh?" Kaze asked.
"What's good? Qadeesha, that's what's good."
"Who the hell is that?" Kaze said puzzled.

Real wrapped his arm around Kaze's shoulder and began telling him everything while they walked to the cafeteria.

As soon as Real and Kaze entered the cafeteria, they spotted Dynasty and Qadeesha sitting directly across from each other at the table in the far right corner. "There they go right there", Real said.

He nodded his head towards where the girls were seated. The two strolled over to the table and sat down on opposite sides from each other.
"What's up", Real greeted smoothly as he scooted closer to Dynasty.

"That's the same thing I'm trying to figure out", Dynasty replied trying her best to hold back her smile.

Oh shit, she's really serious! Real thought to himself.

He took a quick glimpse at Qadeesha and smirked at the sight of his friend putting his thing down. Not even a whole minute passed by and Kaze already had his arm wrapped around Qadeesha's neck, whispering in her ear as she giggled.

"The answer is yes", Real said to Dynasty.

They both just stared at each other for a few seconds without saying anything. Real still couldn't get over the fact that Dynasty really wanted to get with him. He glanced over at the short lunch line then looked back at the three whom he was seated with.

"I'm about to go grab some snacks, do anybody want anything?" He asked while standing up.

"Yeah bro, grab me two packs of butter crunch cookies and some nacho's with cheese", Kaze answered.

"Nah, I'm good", Dynasty said.

"I don't want nothing either Real but thanks anyway", Qadeesha answered.

"Aight" Real said stepping towards the lunch line.

Even though Dynasty and Qadeesha said they didn't want anything, Real still treated them to a few snacks.

Both of Real's hands were filled as he strolled back to the table.

"I got y'all something anyway", he said.

Throughout the rest of the lunch period they all joked, laughed uncontrollably, chit-chatted and got to know one another.

Real and Kaze walked the girls home from school. The two friends walked confidently down the street. They had two of the prettiest girls in the entire school and the fact that they were the ones that came checking for them made it even better!

After making sure their new girls made it home safe, Kaze and Real began walking bck towards the projects.

"Damn Qadeesha sexy as hell!" Kaze said excitedly. "Yeah, I know right! Dynasty bad as hell too, but never mind them for now, we got to hurry up and find Benji so we can get this shit moving", Real said seriously putting business before pleasure.

"Yeah, you right", Kaze agreed.

Real was just as excited as Kaze was about Dynasty and Qadeesha, but his mind was more focused on the money.

"All we got to do is post up in front of Papi's and wait for him to come through. You know he gotta ride through and stunt", Real said.

Once Real and Kaze reached their end of the Boulevard they posted up in front of the drug store, which was across the street from the corner deli. Thirty minutes or so later, Benji's Benz was gliding down the Boulevard with

the Lox song, *'Fuck You'* blaring through the speakers.

"There go Benji right there", Kaze said pointing at his car.

Real saw Benji's Benz and stepped in the middle of the street.

"Yo, Benji!" Real yelled flagging down his car.

The Benz slowed down then came to a stop right next to Real. A thick grey cloud of smoke slowly bellowed out of the window as it was rolled down.

"What's good li'l bruh?" Benji asked while turning down the volume. He hung his head out the window with a blunt dangling from his mouth.

"I gotta holla at you about something. It's important", Real told him looking directly into his blood shot eyes.

"Get in", Benji commanded as he unlocked the door.

Real turned around to look at Kaze who stood in front of the drug store with his back against

the window. "Im'a be right back my nigga", Real assured.

Kaze nodded his head as he watched Real run to the passenger side door and climb inside.

"Oh shit, what's this?" Real said as he sat down on something hard.

He lifted up a little and pulled a black 40 caliber handgun with a red laser from underneath. His eyes grew wide in awe.
"Oh shit", he said again as he held the weapon in his hand examining it.
"Give me this!" Benji exclaimed snatching the gun out of Real's hand and placing it on his lap.

Benji was so high out of his mind that he forgot about the gun he placed on the passenger seat. Benji drove all the way down to the end of the Boulevard, turned down a side street and parked. He leaned back in his seat, took a pull on his blunt, and blew out a thick cloud of smoke. He kept one eye on his

rear view mirror, making sure no one was trying to creep up on him from behind.
"So what you want to talk about that's so important?"

Real let out a deep breath.
"Man, I need some work", he said seriously.

Benji burst out laughing.
"Man, I ain't giving ya li'l young ass no work! What makes you think I'm the nigga you need to holla at for work anyway?"
"Come on man, I'm young but I'm not stupid you know. Ray Charles could see you the nigga to holla at if you trying to get put on."

Real saw that Benji was shaking his head in disapproval.

"For real though big bro, I really need it. Look at the bullshit I got to wear to school!"

Real sat his book bag on his lap and pulled out the ugly PAY-LESS outfits his grandmother brought him. "My nigga Kaze let me borrow his clothes so I wouldn't have

to wear this bullshit", he explained while handing one of the outfits to Benji.

Benji examined the clothes, while Real began talking nonstop.
"If I dress like that to school I'll be laughed at for the rest of my life! My moms survived an overdose of heroin so she in rehab now. My pops got killed the same day I was born", Real told him.

A feeling of empathy came over Benji. His mind flashed back to when he was around Real's age experiencing somewhat of the same struggles. His mother died from AIDS when he was 9 and he never knew who his father was, so he had to make a way for himself in the cold streets of Trenton just like Real was trying to do now.

Benji snapped out of his trance when he heard Real say, "If you don't give me some work, I'm just going to get it from SOMEWHERE else…"
"Listen, this what I'm going to do."

Real quickly sealed his lips and waited eagerly to see what was about to roll off of Benji's tongue.

"I'm going to give you some work and let you pump on my block. But soon as you fuck up one time, I'm cutting ya li'l ass off!" Benji explained seriously handing Real's clothes back to him.

"I ain't gon' fuck up!" Real assured, feeling relieved. "Aight, we gon' handle everything tomorrow. Where you want me to drop you off at? Back in front of the drug store?"
"Yeah."

Benji pulled up in front of the drug store. Real saw Kaze standing in the same spot waiting patiently. Real turned back and looked at Benji who was already looking at him.
"Aight big bruh, I'm a see you tomorrow", Real stated before he climbed out the Benz.
"Aight, stay on top of yourself."

Real closed the passenger door and walked towards Kaze.

"So what did he say?", Kaze asked anxiously, slapping hands with Real.

"It's on. He told me he gon' come holla at me tomorrow."

CHAPTER 9

Benji opened the front door to the stash house and stepped inside. Real was right behind him.
"Lock the door and come in the kitchen", Benji directed.

Real closed and locked the door. He walked into the kitchen and sat down at a glass table.

"I don't know what you sat down for!" Benji snapped.

He opened the cabinet door under the sink and grabbed a digital scale, a plastic bag filled with coke, and a box of plastic wrap. He placed everything on the glass table before stepping over to the sink where he began filling a pot with some water.

Once the pot filled with the proper amount of water Benji turned the water off and walked to the stove. "Hand me the baking soda from the refrigerator and that coke from off the table", he instructed.

Benji placed the pot on the stove and turned the burner on. Real quickly got up from his seat to grab both ingredients.

"Here, Benji."

"Stay right here, and pay close attention because I'm only going to show you this one time."

Benji began to pour half the bag of coke and a decent amount of baking soda in the pot.

"That looks like a hundred grams right there." Benji said under his breath before placing the bag of coke and baking soda on the side of the stove.

Benji was selling coke for so long his eyes were almost as accurate as a digital scale. He grabbed a silver spoon from out one of the dirty pots stacked on the counter and began whipping up. Real watched with wide eyes and listened with open ears as Benji explained every method there was to know about cooking coke. The way he smiled while stirring you could tell that he really took pride in his work and enjoyed doing it.

Within minutes, the liquid turned into a hard crystal-like rocks. Benji picked the pot up by the handle and walked over to the glass table. He used the spoon to scrape out every single crumb of freebase from inside the pot on to a glass plate. As it cooled, he cut it into rocks until every single crumb was hardened. He dropped it onto the scale and it read a 120 grams. "Just like I thought", he said as he put the free base inside the saran wrap, and then tied it in a knot.

Benji looked at Real standing next to him.
"It ain't a nigga in this city that can cook coke better than me. I hope you been paying attention because it's your turn to whip up."

Benji nodded his head towards the stove. "Go head!"

Even though Real paid close attention to Benji's
instructions the thought of making a mistake made him feel a bit uneasy.

Real grabbed the pot from off the table and headed towards the sink. First, he filled the pot with water then went over to the stove to turn on the fire. He picked up the bag of coke and box of baking soda and poured it into the pot. He picked up the spoon and began stirring, repeating everything he saw Benji do. Before he knew it, the cocaine liquid had turned hard.

Real picked the pot up and walked to the table where he carefully scraped the free base on to the plate carefully.
"So how did I do?"
"We 'bout to find out right now."

Benji picked up Real's mix and placed it on the digital scale and it read 90 grams, causing him to smirk.
"Shit, you did way better than I thought you would. The first time I cooked up I fucked up my whole hundred gram pack! So for you to only loose 10 grams out of a hundred tells me you a fast learner."

Benji placed the 2nd batch of crack in a plastic bag and tied it in a knot and handed both plastic packs of crack to Real.

"That's 210 grams. Now sit down for a minute."

Real sat down and looked up at Benji. For the next 3 hours Benji drilled the do's and don't's of the game in Real's head. He repeatedly explained the prices for the fiends and the wholesale prices for the corner hustlers. He also taught him how to work the scale. Real soaked up all the information and advice like a sponge. He couldn't wait to see what the game (which was really no game at all) had to offer.

Benji pulled up and parked his Benz in the front entrance of the Gut side of Donnelly Homes projects. Real didn't want Benji to drop him off near his grandmother's building just in case she was looking out the window. She would've flipped if she saw him getting out of the neighborhood drug dealer's car! "Aight lil bro, I'll see you in a few days."
"Aight", Real stated.

The two slapped hands. As soon as Real hopped out the car he began speed walking through the projects. School let out about 5 hours ago, and Real wasn't trying to be any later than he already was. He knew his grandmother was going to be tripping no matter what excuse he gave her.

Real entered his building and darted up the steps sliding the key in the door. As he opened the door and stepped inside the apartment, he saw his grandmother sitting on the couch with her arms folded across her chest with a sheet of paper in her hand.

"What the hell is this?!" Candace yelled, handing Real the paper.

Real read the paper as if he had no clue of what was going on. It was a letter from the Board of Education informing Candace that Real was picked up from the streets during school hours. *How the fuck did they find out when we gave them fake names?* He thought.

Candace was staring him down, she was so disappointed.

"All I asked was for you to do good in school!"

"But grandma..."

"I don't want to hear nothing ya li'l bad ass got to say! You're on punishment until I say you're off. Now go in that damn room and stay in there!"

Real stormed to his room, closed the door behind him, and dove into the bed. He let out a deep sigh as he lay sprawled out on the bed staring up at the ceiling. He had already knew that if he was caught that meant Kaze was too. *Damn, how am I gonna get rid of the coke if I'm on punishment?* He thought to himself pissed off.

Real fought his sleep for about an hour before he finally dozed off thinking about how Benji would look at him if he was to fuck up or be late with his first package. Even though he was a new jack to the game, he knew that not having the money on time was surely bad for business.

A few hours later, Real's sleepy eyes finally opened. He lazily slid out of bed and started making his way to the bathroom. Before he reached the bathroom, he looked into the living room and noticed that the TV and kitchen light was off. *Grandma must be out gambling somewhere*, Real thought to himself.

Real flushed the toilet, washed his hands, and walked into the living room where he opened the window. He leaned forward to look down at Kaze's living room, which was across the walkway.

"Kaze!" Real yelled, trying not to be too loud.

Within seconds Kaze's living room window opened and his head popped out. Real could tell by the look on his face that he was caught too.

"I'm on punishment!"

"Me too! Ya mom home?"

"Nah, she went grocery shopping like 10 minutes ago."

"Hurry up and come over!" Real urged.

By the time Real grabbed an apple out of the refrigerator, Kaze walked through the door.
"So how did everything go with you and Benji?"
"Everything went good! He fronted us some work so we can get on our feet", Real replied while chewing on his apple.

They were standing face to face in the living room near the front door.

"That's what the fuck I'm talking about!"
"Hold on real quick."

Real walked quickly to his room. When he came back into the living room he was carrying his book bag. He sat down on the couch, placed what was left of his chewed up apple on the table, and unzipped the book bag. Real pulled out a digital scale and the two plastic bags filled with crack.

"Damn Benji hit you heavy huh", Kaze said as he examined the two plastic bags of crack.
"Yea, I guess so. Benji said he was gon' be back to holla at me in a couple of days to pick

138

the bread up. But we both on punishment so it's gonna be impossible to have this finished by then."

Real let out a deep sigh and ran his hand across the top of his head.
"Damn man! I gave Benji my word I was going to make it happen."
"That's what we gon' do then! I don't know why you soundin' all sad and shit. All we got to do is take turns going to trap whenever one of our peoples leaves the house."

Real thought about what Kaze was saying and slowly nodded his head in agreement.
"Yeah, you right, that's how we moving then."
"Let's go get this fucking money!" Kaze exclaimed standing up.
"Hold up bro, sit back down and listen to what I'm about to say to you."

Kaze sat back down and looked at Real.

"Since this is our first time we're only taking one bag of the work with us and then we'll see how it go from there."

"Aight.", Kaze said nodding his head.

For the next 30 minutes, Kaze listened intently as Real briefly explained the prices and the do's and don't's of the game just as it was told to him.

It was pitch black and windy outside. Real and Kaze got near the other end of the projects when they stopped in their tracks and began observing their surroundings. They noticed the busted lights on the red brick walls above some of the entry doors, which added an ominous vibe to the scenery. They also noticed the fiends that stood around in separate little groups looking like they were waiting for someone to come through with some freebase. Real turned to face Kaze.

"One of us gon be the lookout directing the traffic, while the other is inside the hallway serving the fiends."

"Sounds like a plan. Come on", Kaze agreed.

Real stepped towards Building #3 while Kaze posted up in the center of the projects near the entrance gate to get a view of who and what was coming in and out. Kaze looked around and noticed that none of the fiends were paying him any mind.

Kaze heard foot steps coming from behind and quickly turned to see a tall dark skin man with a bald head walking towards him. Kaze stared into the fiend's face who continued past him as if he didn't see him standing there.
"I got what you looking for", Kaze stated.

The fiend stopped and quickly turned around.

"What you say youngin?"
"You heard me, I got what you need."

The fiend approached him.

"Hold up, I ain't got it on me. My peoples got it in Building #3."

Kaze extended his arm motioning for the tall man to stop. The dark skin man turned around and began speed walking towards the building and shot up the first flight of stairs where he was served by Real. The fiend sped out of the building with the freebase cuffed in his hand. He made sure to let all the other fiends standing around know that crack was being sold out of Building #3.

Several different crowds of fiends immediately bum rushed the building from all angles. For the next 30 minutes, fiends ran in and out of the building while Kaze directed traffic. Every pocket in Real's jeans was stuffed with crumpled up money as he quickly strolled out of the building and approached Kaze.

Real's heart was beating rapidly, he caught an adrenaline rush from all the fast money that was coming at him back to back.
"What's wrong?" Kaze asked.
"I'm done! That's what's wrong."
"You sold all that shit that fast?"

"Yeah, now let's go to the crib, count this money and grab some more work."

The two made it to Real's grandmother's apartment, counted and stashed the money, grabbed the other plastic bag of work, and rushed out the door.

Once Real and Kaze made it to the other side of the projects it was the same procedure, Kaze watched while Real served. The only thing that changed was the crowd. A whole twenty minutes had gone by, and not one fiend had come inside the hallway to be served. Frustrated, Real stepped out of the building and walked towards Kaze.

"Damn a sale ain't come through here yet. Where did all the fiends go?"

"They keep going in Building #7. I tried to stop them but they ignored me and just kept it moving."

Real turned around and saw two fiends speed walking out of Building #7.

"Man, come on!"

CARDE'L

Real and Kaze entered Building #7 and began walking up the stairwell. They noticed that there were fiends lined up from the second floor all the way up to the third floor waiting to be served.

"Damn, whoever this nigga is got every fiend in the city coming to see him", Real said as he and Kaze made their way to the top of the third floor.

The middle door opened and a young boy stood in the doorway holding a plastic bag of crack in his hand. He was light skin, slim, and rocked a low cut Caesar.

"Look who we have here, Motherfucking Real!" The kid said with a smile emphasizing every word.

He noticed the confused look that appeared on Real's face, and chuckled.

"I'm Dose, Benji my man. He let me know you was gon' be out here doing ya thing. The only problem is you ain't gon' be able to sell a crumb of crack while I'm out here!"

144

Dose definitely didn't lie when he told Real he wouldn't be able to sell a crumb of crack. He had clientele that was out of this world. Every young hustler in the area hated when he showed up on the scene because their money flow did a 360 and went right in to the palms of Dose's hands. It was to the point where some fiends didn't even cop if he wasn't out hustling. Dose's only problem was that he never stacked his money, the nigga spent it just as fast as he made it.

Real and Kaze looked at each other, knowing that they didn't stand a chance. Dose finally finished serving the fiends, stuffing the money in his front pockets. He turned to look at Real and Kaze.
"Come inside."

Dose closed the door, locked it, and led them to the kitchen. They all grabbed a seat at a circular wooden table.
"Come on Dose, you could at least let me finish half of what I got left so I can make it to the crib before it's too late", Real pleaded.

145

He watched as Dose pulled out the wads of crumbled up money from his pocket and placed it on the table.

"What's half of what you got left?" Dose asked.

"Sixty", Real replied.

"Sixty?" Dose repeated with raised eyebrows.

Dose stopped everything he was doing and looked at Real.

"You mean sixty grams?" he asked in disbelief.

"Yeah."

So if that's half, this li'l nigga must've had a hundred and twenty grams. It took me a whole year and a half for Benji to front me that much work, Dose thought to himself.

"How much work you got left?" Real asked.

"10 grams."

"Listen man, I know you need some more coke with all this money that's coming your way. Buy these 100 grams off me."

Dose's blood began boiling inside. *Yeah right. What I look like letting this lil nigga that just came off the porch serve me,* he thought.

"Nah, I'm good. I'm gon' just holla at Benji", he said letting his pride get in the way.

Dose pulled out his cell phone and dialed Benji's number. He felt dumb and disappointed when his call went straight to voicemail. Dose called a few more times but still didn't get an answer. He put his phone back in his pocket and sighed out loud, obviously frustrated.
"Yo, let me get a hundred grams off you. How much you going to charge me, 25 a gram right?"
"Nah, but you can get it for 28 though."

For the next 10 minutes Dose tried talking Real down on his price, but he was unable to get it off. After serving Dose, Real counted the money with a feeling of relief. He already made the money he owed to Benji and a

decent amount of money for him and Kaze to split.

"Aight, my nigga, we about to blow this joint", Real said.

He and Kaze got up from their seats and slapped hands with Dose, then they both headed out the front door.

CHAPTER 10

Real and Kaze skipped their last period class and went downtown to purchase some new clothes. They made sure to make it back in time to meet up with their girlfriends after school let out. Real and Kaze hugged their girls and held their hands as they walked down the street on their way to Dynasty's house.

"Oh y'all went shopping huh?" Dynasty said looking down at the bags.

"Yeah you know a nigga gotta stay fly", Real said smiling.

"I know y'all bought us something."

Without saying a word, Real looked at Kaze who was walking behind him. Dynasty noticed the *Oops I forgot* look on Real's face and snapped her teeth.

"Get off me", she said with an attitude.

Dynasty snatched her hand away from his grasp and stormed off. Qadeesha looked down at Kaze's bag then looked up.

"Baby, I know you bought me something, right?"

She already knew the answer, but she wanted to hear what Kaze was going to say.

"Um..I ain't know ya clothes or ya shoe size", Kaze made excuses.
"You would've known if you asked when you saw me during lunch. I'm quite sure y'all already had plans to leave before then."
"Nah, we ain't even know we were leaving when I saw you."
"Stop lying nigga!"

Qadeesha also snatched her hand away and began speed walking to catch up to her big cousin. Real and Kaze both shook their heads.

"Man they tripping", Kaze said.
"I know, right?" Real agreed.

Real and Kaze tried to calm their girlfriends down the entire walk home, but it ended unsuccessfully with the door slamming in

their faces. Real wanted so badly to knock on the door but his pride wouldn't let him.

"Fuck it then, let's go holla at Benji so we can get some more work", Real said with an attitude stepping off of the porch.

Kaze nodded his head in agreement while thinking to himself what he was going to do with Qadeesha.

As soon as Real and Kaze got near the Gut side of the projects they spotted Benji's car parked in front of the school.

"Lets hurry up and get to this nigga car before he pull off", Real said.

While Real approached the car, Kaze strolled across the street and posted up in front of the project entrance gate. Real began tapping on the passenger's side window. Benji had his head down counting the money he just collected from his workers. When he saw that it was Real he unlocked the door. Real climbed inside the Benz.

"Ok, I see you just came from picking that fly shit out", said Benji.

"Yeah. I wanted to let you know I finished what you gave me and need some more work ASAP!"

Real dug his hands into his front pockets and pulled out two wads of cash. Benji's beamed like a proud dad.
"Damn! This li'l nigga done with that shit I gave him already. It ain't even been a full twenty-four hours yet!"

Benji took the two wads of cash and added it to his pile.

"Say no more, I'm about to go grab something for you know."
"Aight, I'ma be waiting right here", Real said .
He grabbed his bags and climbed out of the car, then walked across the street to tell Kaze.

CHAPTER 11

A year and a half had passed, allowing Real and Kaze to develop an inseparable bond. The two friends never looked back since the day Benji fronted them their first package. They spent every single day together going hard in the hood and considered themselves brothers from another mother.

Although Real was younger than Kaze, he had more leadership qualities. He was quiet, calm, and very smart for his age. His was more about getting money, but when it was time to bust his gun he enjoyed doing that too. Kaze, known as Kamikaze in the streets now, was what you would call a certified problem. Real gave him this nickname because of his *I don't give a fuck* attitude and reckless behavior. He lived for drama and got a kick out of doing whatever he wanted to people.

Real cut his last period class to go gamble inside the bathroom along with Kaze, who didn't gamble at all. Real picked up a

gambling habit out of no where, perhaps it was just hereditary.

"Head!" Real shouted in a tone high while throwing the dice against the bathroom wall.

Real was holding a wad of cash in his hand while Kaze stood with his back against the wall rolling up a blunt watching the dice game. The four young boys standing over top of the rolling dice were looking down anxiously, as 4-4-5 appeared on them. They were playing Ceelo and Real had bank, which meant that everyone had to shoot to the numbers he rolled.

"Shoot to my star!" Real stated confidently.

He moved to the side so one of the young boys could shoot to the number he just rolled. Just as the young boy picked up the dice, shook them, and threw them against the wall, the security guards Darrell and Terrence walked through the door.
"Well look what we have here!" Darrell shouted.

Darrell and his partner stood near the sink looking directly at the 5 boys. Everyone except Real immediately became nervous.

Damn they must have heard us, Real mumbled to himself. He approached Darrell while still holding the wad of cash in his hand.
"Let me holla at you", Real said tapping Darrell on the chest with the money.

The two exited the bathroom. Darrell looked at Terrence.
"Don't let none of these li'l mufuckas run out this bathroom."

Real and Darrell stood face to face in the hallway.
"I got three hundred for you if you just let us finish", Real said trying to bribe him.

Darrell looked at Real like he lost his mind.

"What the hell I look like?" Darrell said.
"Aight man, five hundred. I ain't going no higher that's, more than half your pay check."

Darrell glanced at the cash in his hand and Real knew he had him right where he wanted him.
"Come on man before somebody sees us", Real urged.

He took five crispy hundred dollar bills from the wad and handed it to Darrell. Darrell looked around and cautiously surveyed the hallway before stuffing the money in his pocket.

Real didn't really care about the money because he was already up 3 grand. He walked back into the bathroom.
"Shit, don't stop nigga. Shoot the dice!"

Kaze and the young boys looked at him with confused expressions on their faces.
"What you can't hear nigga? Shoot the dice", Real ordered.

Real saw Terrence walk out of the bathroom from the corner of his eye. The other young boys picked the dice up, shook them, and

threw them against the wall. The dice game continued for some time. Real walked away with all four of the young boy's money in his Gucci pants pockets talking slick.

Kaze pulled up in front of the school yard in Real's blue Cadillac Deville. Qadeesha jumped in the passenger seat while Real and Dynasty climbed in the back. Kaze had his own car but he always drove Real's. He liked it plus Real hadn't learned how to drive yet!
"I stuck the shit out of them niggas", Real bragged.

He dug in his pocket and pulled out the four grand he won at the dice game and looked at Dynasty.
"So you already know what that mean right?"
"Nah Real, what does it mean?" Dynasty asked.
"It means we're all going to Philly to shop! Everything on me!"

Dynasty's face lit up. Ever since Dynasty had showed her ass the time Real went shopping for himself and ain't get her anything he

always made sure he spoiled her with gifts. Kamikaze was the same exact way with Qadeesha.

"Before we go, I gotta go on the other end of the Boulevard to pick this bread up real quick", Kaze said as he sped off.

Kaze loved driving fast especially when the girls were in the car. He got a kick out of seeing how scared they reacted.

"Boy if you don't slow down!" Qadeesha screamed fastening her seat belt.

Real and Kaze both burst into laughter.

"Ain't nothing funny!" Dynasty co-signed as she too fastened her seat belt.

Kaze flew down the Boulevard like it was the highway. Once he reached his destination, Kaze slammed on the breaks and parked the car on the side of the curb. He climbed out and walked to the crowd of young boys standing on the corner in front of the deli. *Where the fuck is this nigga at?* Kaze said to himself scanning the crowd visibly agitated.

Just as Kaze was about to walk in the deli, the person he was looking for came walking out.
"Just who I was looking for, my nigga Baby Boy", Kaze stopped him in his tracks.

Kaze looked at Baby Boy from head to feet, admiring his purple and white Gucci sneakers with the jacket and hat to match.

"I see you out here fresh to death, so I know you got that bread right by now."
"Nah Kaze, I ain't done yet. Give me like two more days!" Baby Boy said dryly looking down at the ground.

Kamikaze frowned, he couldn't believe Baby Boy was trying to give him the run around.
"Two more days? I gave you almost an extra two weeks! What the fuck this look like Burger King?"

Kaze forcefully grabbed Baby Boy by his jacket and pulled a chrome .357 Magnum off his waist. Baby Boy's eyes widened as he shook uncontrollably.

"Oh shit, please don't kill me. My nigga I'm gon' have ya money before the day over!"

Kamikaze swung his arm violently smacking Baby Boy in the mouth with the butt of the gun.
"Agghh!" Baby Boy yelled out in agony as he spit his teeth out along with a thick glob of blood.
"Have it ya way, huh? Well this is Kamikaze way!"

Kaze glanced at the crowd of young boys who stood by with shocked looks on their faces. Kaze continued to pistol whip Baby Boy relentlessly.

"Please Kaze. I'm sorry, I'm gon' pay you!" Baby Boy cried through the gushing blood in agony as it began to spatter all over his clothes.

Every time Kaze hit him with the butt of the gun, a different color appeared on Baby Boy's light skin. Screaming and hollering, he tried

desperately to break loose from Kamikaze's strong grasp but couldn't.

Qadeesha, Real, and Dynasty were watching from the car the whole time.
"Real, hurry up and go get Kaze before he kill that boy!" Qadeesha yelled in a panic.
"Hurry up baby. Go 'head!" Dynasty demanded urgently pushing Real on the shoulder.

Real finally climbed out of the Cadillac and darted towards Kaze. By then Kaze had the barrel of the gun down Baby Boy's throat.
"Strip muhfucka, take off everything!"

Cars rode pass slowly, looking at the scene out of their car windows shocked at what they were witnessing. Unable to see straight, Baby Boy took off all his bloody clothes and was completely naked standing on the corner of the Boulevard with his hands covering his private area. The cold concrete caused his feet to feel numb instantly as the strong wind blew making sure it's presence was felt. Baby Boy started shivering uncontrollably.

"Kaze fall back! It's too many people out here!" Real commanded authoritatively as he approached his brother from another mother.

Kaze heard Real's voice and quickly snapped out of the homicidal zone he was caught up in.

"If I ever see you out here trapping after today you a dead man. You hear me?" Kaze threatened through clenched teeth.
"Um hum..."
"Now get the fuck out of here!"

Without looking back, Baby Boy ran off as fast as he could down the Boulevard completely naked. Dynasty and Qadeesha, watched everything as it played out from the car. Worried looks turned into smiles and laughter.
"Oh so that's why they call him Baby Boy", Qadeesha said.
"Why?" Dynasty asked.
"Because he got a baby dick!"

They both were laughing when Real and Kamikaze got back into the car. They then sped off on their way to Philly.

Once they arrived in Philly they shopped until they dropped up and down South Street, ate until their belly's felt like they were going to explode, and then headed home to Dynasty's house where they would spend all night because her aunt Carmen was on vacation.

With both hands filled with shopping bags, Dynasty held the door open with her foot as Real, Kaze, and Qadeesha walked inside the apartment and sat on the green leather couches in the living room. Dynasty headed to her room in the back. Real leaned forward to grab the remote control that rested on the oval shaped glass table.
"Babes can you grab me something to drink when you get a chance", Real shouted loud enough so Dynasty could hear him.

Real turned on the TV and began flicking through the channels. This was Real's second

time in Dynasty's aunt's apartment. He always tried to come over and spend time with her, but Dynasty wouldn't let him. She would always tell him to meet her at Qadeesha's house. She was too afraid of being caught by her strict aunt. Aunt Carmen didn't like anyone in her apartment when she wasn't there, especially not a young thug that was knee deep into the streets like Real.

Qadeesha and Kaze were on the couch across from Real, passionately kissing and gently rubbing all over each other's bodies. Dynasty stepped in the kitchen where she poured Real a glass of orange juice then strutted in the living room.
"Huh baby, it's nice and cold for you too."

Dynasty looked at Qadeesha and Kaze who were now on the couch grinding.
"Damn, y'all just can't wait huh?"

Dynasty chuckled as she strolled over to the stereo system next to the TV. She turned the volume all the way up to the max after hearing her favorite song by Ashanti. Dynasty

glided down the hall into the bathroom singing the lyrics word for word.

"Hold on baby, let me get fresh and change up", Qadeesha whispered as she took her tongue out of Kaze's mouth.

She stood up and walked down the hall. Kaze's lustful eyes followed her.

"I'm gon' bust her ass tonight", Kaze said excitedly with a wide grin on his face.

Qadeesha had him waiting for months, and now he was finally about to get some.

"Kaze, you ever had sex before?" Real asked.
"Nah."
"So how you so sure you're going to bust her ass?" Real asked chuckling.
"Because I been studying pornos."
"You shot the fuck out bruh!"

Real was a virgin too and was just as excited as Kaze was. He just managed to keep his composure which was something he was always good at no matter the circumstances.

CHAPTER 12

Real woke up from the sound of his phone vibrating on the dresser next to the bed. He rolled over to answer.

"Yo", Real said half asleep.

"Damn boy what you was doing? I called you like three times already", Tadasia replied.

"I was sleep."

"They didn't have the car you wanted at the rental spot so I got you something different. You gon' like it."

"What is it?"

"You'll see when you get here. Grandma called me last night worried sick about you, she said you didn't come home last night."

Real slightly shook his head and sighed. He glanced at Dynasty who was lying next to him moving around under the covers.

"Aight, I'll be over there in like 10 minutes", Real said yawning.

"Aight, love you", Tadasia said before hanging up.

Real swiftly removed the sheets that covered his naked body, and slid out of the bed to put his clothes on. Dynasty looked up at him as she sat up in the bed.

"Who was that and where the hell you think you're going?"

"That was my sister telling me to come pick up the rental car me and Kaze rented."

Real began tying his blue and white Jordan's.

"I wanna come", Dynasty said in an innocent tone. "I'm coming back to get you as soon as I come from my grandma's spot."

Knowing where the conversation was heading, Real darted out the room before Dynasty could respond. *It's too early in the morning to be arguing,* he thought to himself. As soon as he opened the bedroom door where Kaze and Qadeesha was Real saw Kaze in a deep sleep snoring and wrapped up under the covers with Qadeesha.

"Kaze wake up."

Real walked over to the bed tapping him on the shoulder.

"Huh?" Kaze rolled over to see Real who was standing over top of them.
"Hurry up and get up. We got to go get the rental from my sister. She said they didn't have the truck so she got something else."

Kaze quickly got out of the bed and slipped into his clothes. They both made their way out the door and on their way to Tadasia's apartment.

When Kaze pulled into the projects, they spotted an all black four door Porsche parked in front of Tadasia's building.
"That must be what she rented right there", Real said.

Kaze parked, and the two hopped out of the Cadillac.

"Damn that thang look like a jet on wheels!" Kaze said in amazement as they approached the vehicle examining it inside and out. When

Kaze saw the two hundred + gauge on the speedometer his adrenaline began to rush. He couldn't wait to take it for a spin and see what it felt like to open it up on the highway.

"What are we waiting for? Let's go get the keys!" Kaze stated.
"Come on!" Real responded.

They darted up the three flights of steps to Tadasia's. Real turned the door knob to see if it was unlocked and it was so he opened it and they walked inside. "Why you got the door unlocked?" Real asked looking at his sister like she was crazy.

He and Kaze stood by the large fish tank. Tadasia was sitting on her black leather couch with her boyfriend Omar seated on the floor in between her legs braiding his hair in cornrows.
"Boy calm down, ain't nobody coming up in here. I unlocked it because I knew you was on your way. I know y'all saw the car parked in front of the building. Do y'all like it?"

"Hell yeah we like it! Every bad broad in the city gon' be trying to dive in our drawls when they see us come through in that space ship!"

Tadasia and Omar laughed.
"That's until they find out how old y'all little asses are!" Tadasia giggled.
"Where the keys?" Real asked.
"They're in my room on the dresser."

Real grabbed the keys from off the dresser. He felt his phone vibrating in his pocket as he walked back into the living room.
"Yo?" Real answered.
"What's good lil bro, it's Benji. I need a big favor from you."
"Let me know what it is and it's done."
"I need you to go to 136 Walnut Avenue and holla at my peoples. He gon' have something for you." "Aight, say no more. I'm on my way out there right now."

Real walked back in to the living room.
"That was Benji. He want me to go on Walnut and grab something for him", Real told Kaze.

"Give me the keys and come on then", Kaze demanded.

Real and Kaze rushed out of the apartment. Tadasia yelled out to Real.
"I think grandma at Bingo, call her and let her know you're alright!"

Real and Kaze jumped into the Porsche and sped out of the projects. All eyes were on them as they cruised through the city on their way to pick up whatever it was Benji had waiting for them.

Kaze pulled up to the address and threw the car in park. Real looked at Kaze.
"I'll be right back."
"Man you sure you don't want me to come inside with you?" Kaze asked feeling uncomfortable about Real going inside the beat up looking house by himself.
"Yeah, I'm good bruh. I'm gon' just grab it and come right back out."

Real hopped out of the Porsche. He looked around surveying his surroundings as he

stepped on the raggedy porch and knocked on the door. KNOCK! KNOCK! KNOCK!

"Who is it", a male voice asked.
"It's Real."

Real heard the bolts on the door being unlocked before the door finally swung open. A brown skin young man with a nappy afro stood in the entry way. He stepped to the side so Real could come in.
"Go in the kitchen."

Real cautiously stepped inside and walked straight toward the kitchen. The young man with the nappy afro closed the door, locked it, and followed behind him.

Once inside the kitchen, Real observed a Mac 10 machine gun and a black duffle bag on the table. There was a young man seated at the table with a smirk on his face.
"Real what's good my nigga. I'm Snake Eyes. You got here kinda quick."

He stood up from his seat and held his hand out. Snake Eyes was brown skin and tall, slim with long cornrows. His slanted eyes gave him a sly look which matched his demeanor. He was only 17, but the long hard six years he spent running the streets had him looking a decade older.

Snake Eyes was the only person Benji dealt with outside of his own area. And since Benji supplied him with the best coke in town, Snake Eyes had majority of his 'hood in the palm of his hand with a team full of wolves that would do any and everything he told them to do.

Real looked down at Snake Eyes hand for a few seconds before he shook it. Real didn't care what his name was he was just there to get whatever he had for Benji.
"Time is money and I ain't trying to waste a second, nor dollar."

Snake Eyes nodded his head. *He's just how Benji said he was*, Snake Eyes thought to himself. "I know that's right", he said.

Real turned and looked down at the machine gun and duffle bag that rested on the table.

"So is this what I came to pick up?"
"Yeah. That's $35k in the bag. Tell Benji that I'll have the rest for him in a week, tops", Snake Eyes assured. "Aight, I'll let him know."

Real grabbed the duffle bag off the table and made his way out of the house.

Kaze popped the trunk when he saw Real come out the house. Real quickly put the duffle bag in the trunk and climbed inside the Porsche. Kaze pulled out and started heading back to the projects. Real pulled his cell phone out to dial Benji's number.
"Yo, whats up?" Benji answered.
"Big bruh, everything everything. What you want me to do now?"
"Just hold it for now. Do you think you can handle that?"

Real looked at his watch and saw that it was 1:30PM. He knew that his grandmother usually went to Bingo at 12:00 noon and wouldn't be in the house.

"Yeah, I can handle it."
"When I need it, I'll call you and let you know.", Benji told him before hanging up.

When he reached home, Real put his ear to the door. He held the duffle bag tightly in his hand. He didn't hear the TV, nor any movement inside the apartment, so he quickly pulled the key out of his pocket and went in.
"Boy where the hell you been at?!" Candace screamed from the kitchen catching Real by surprise.

Candace knew Real was going to slide in and out thinking she wasn't going to be there, so she decided not to go to Bingo. Real's eyes popped at the sight of his grandmother getting out of the chair and walking towards him.
"I stayed the night at Kaze's house!" He lied.
"You a damn lie!"

Candace was now standing face to face with Real in the living room.

"I went across the walkway and talked to Carla and she said she ain't see you nor Kaze all night!" Candace looked down at the duffle bag in Real's hand. He noticed the look of discomfort on Real's face and immediately grew suspicious.

"What the hell is that you got inside of that bag?" She asked.

"It's some clothes", Real replied nervously.

"I don't believe you! Open it and let me see!"

Real swallowed hard as his heart beat rapidly.

"It's my clothes grandma!"

"If it's just your clothes then open it!"

Not knowing what to say or do, Real just stood there with a blank look on his face as if he didn't hear what his grandmother had commanded him to do.

"As long as you live under my roof you're going to listen to what the hell I tell you to do. You're still a child boy now open it!"

Real sighed out loud as he looked down at the floor.

"Give me this shit."

Candace tried to snatch the bag out of Real's hand to open it, but only unzipped it halfway before Real snatched it back out of her hand. They both tugged back and forth over the duffle bag causing the wrapped up rubber band wads of cash to fall out of the bag on to the floor.

Candace let go of the bag and gasped at the sight of the wads of cash falling to the floor. "Where in the hell did you get all this money from?"

She realized that all of the rumors her gambling partners told her about her grandson living the street life were true. Without saying one word, Real quickly

dropped down to pick up the bundles of cash from off the ground.

"Get the hell out of my apartment. Right now! You think you a grown man, so I'm gon' treat you like one."

Real darted into the back room and came back out with a gym bag filled with the 20 grand that he had saved. In the opposite hand he held the duffle bag. Candace's eyes moistened as she watched Real rush out the door. She wasn't just feeling hurt inside, she was devastated. She couldn't believe Real would disrespect her apartment by bringing drug money and no telling what else in to her home. It also hurt her heart to finally know for sure that her 14 year old grandson was living the vicious lifestyle that swallowed his father.

Candace walked to the kitchen window where she peeked out the blinds and saw Real getting into the expensive car. She grabbed the cordless phone from the kitchen table and began dialing furiously.

Real slammed the passenger door and placed the duffle bag and gym bag in the backseat. Kaze could tell by the expression on his face that something went wrong.

"What happened?"

"My grandma tried to snatch the bag from me. But I snatched it back and the money fell out", Real said sadly.

He felt bad about the the tug-of-war with his grandmother over the duffle bag. Kaze's eyes grew as wide as 2 fifty cent pieces

"Word up? What did she say?!"

"What did she say? Nigga she kicked me the fuck out!"

"Damn bruh…!"

"I ain't worried though, take me back to my sister's spot. I'm about to ask her if I can move in."

"You should leave the money at my crib, ain't no telling what type of shit that nigga Omar be on", Kaze advised.

Real thought about it for a few seconds.

"Nah, I'm good, that nigga know better. Plus ain't nobody gon' know it's there."

"Aight, if you say so", Kaze said with a raised eyebrow.

As Kaze was exiting the Donnelly Homes parking lot turning onto Southard Street, an all black unmarked police car with two detectives inside of it were driving toward them on the opposite side of the street.

"Oh shit, there they go in the black car!" Kaze shouted.

"Chill regular yo. Just chill regular", Real instructed.

Two detectives slowly rode pass intently looking inside the vehicle.

"Damn! They busting a U-Turn!" Kaze yelled while looking through the rear view mirror.

Damn man! I should've just let Kaze put the money in his house, Real thought as his heart beat rapidly. He turned around in his seat and saw the black unmarked car speeding up behind them with their sirens on.

"Hurry up! Hurry up! Make a right turn at the light!"

Kaze made a sharp right turn at the light and then slammed his foot on the gas peddle, causing the black Porsche to shoot down Calhoun Street like a speeding bullet. Struggling to keep up, the unmarked police car gave chase behind them. Kaze saw how fast the needle rose to over hundred plus miles and immediately his adrenaline began pumping! He had been chased by the police a few times, but never in a car as fast as the one he was in now.

Kaze had them by a nice little stretch when he made a reckless right turn down another side street that led to the other side of the projects where Real's big sister lived. He made a left turn into the entrance and immediately slammed on the brakes near the guard booth, causing the car to come to a screeching halt.

Real grabbed the two bags of money, jumped out of the Porsche and ran towards his sister's end of the projects. Kaze hopped out of the

car, and ran off in the opposite direction towards the other end of the projects. By this time, a swarm of patrol cars began pulling up from all angles, surrounding the projects.

A detective driving a Chevy Caprice slammed his foot on the brake peddle, leaving tire marks in the street. When the unmarked car stopped, it bumped into the back of the Porsche and another detective jumped out, not too sure of which one of the young thugs to chase! Both detectives decided to go after Real since he was the one holding the two bags.

Real ran as fast as he could trying to make it to his sister's building, but realized that he wouldn't make it without them seeing exactly which apartment he ran in. So he ran to a building near by and quickly sprinted up all three flights of stairs. As he climbed the ladder that led to the rooftop, he heard the detectives running up the stairway behind him. Holding both bags in each hand, Real ran all the way to the other end on the rooftop and stopped in his tracks on the edge near the fire escape.

"Damn, what I'm gon' do? What I'm gon' do? What I'm gon' do?"

Real began to panic as he looked down at the several patrol cars that surrounded the entire area. The sound of the sirens grew louder and louder by the second. He looked to his left and noticed two green dumpsters next to each other. Real took in a deep breath then exhaled, trying his best to grab hold of his composure. Holding on tight to the duffle bag, and locking his eyes on the dumpster, he began slowly and steadily swinging the bag back and forth before cautiously releasing it from his grasp.

Real desperately hoped that he didn't miss as he watched the duffle bag fall in slow motion! A feeling of relief came over him when he saw that it landed straight into the dumpster! He then threw the other bag into the dumpster before he darted for the roof slot, where he quickly climbed down the ladder into a totally different hallway.

Real ran down the steps to Ms. Gail's apartment on the 2nd floor. She sold hot platters, snacks, and tobacco products to everyone in the 'hood! Knowing that the door would be open, Real walked inside calmly as if he wasn't being chased by the police. "Hey Ms. Gail. Can I get a chicken platter with mac and cheese and some greens? And do you mind if I eat in your kitchen."

Real stood in the living room breathing heavily. Ms. Gail was sitting on her couch watching the news. She quickly got up and began walking into the kitchen. "No, I don't mind baby. It sounds like the whole police force outside! What happened?"

She made Real's plate and sat it on the square wooden kitchen table near the window.

"I'm not sure, but it looked like they were chasing somebody."
"Let me go lock my door before somebody try running up in here!" Ms. Gail said.

Too late for that, Real thought to himself as he picked up a piece of fried chicken from off his plate and bit in to it. Ms. Gail went to the door, locked it, and then stepped back into the kitchen.

"Ms. Gail can I use the bathroom", he asked politely. "Yeah baby, go ahead. First door on the left."

Real stood up, walked into the bathroom, closed the door and sat on the toilet. He took his cell phone from his pocket and dialed Kaze's cell number, but it went straight to voicemail.
"Damn man, they got Kaze!" He mumbled to himself angrily as he clicked off and dialed his sister's house phone.

"Hello", Omar answered.
"Put Tadasia on the phone!"
"She ain't here. She went downtown to cash her check like 15 minutes ago."

Real breathed deeply out of his nose.

"Listen, the police just chased me through the projects I..."

"Oh shit, that was you all them police was chasing after?"

"Yeah...just listen, I need you to go in my sisters room and look out the window and watch the dumpster for me. It's two duffle bags filled with cash inside of them."

Real didn't know if he could trust Omar or not but he didn't have a choice.

"I'm on my way to the window right now", Omar said.

"Oh and hurry up and call Tadasia. Tell her to report the rental car stolen!"

Meanwhile, Kaze was hiding under a big black pick-up truck that was parked at the end of the parking lot near the park. He could see the tires of the several cop cars and the shoes of officers that were searching the area for him.

"He's got to be in this area somewhere. We just saw him!" One of the officers yelled. "Check in those buildings over there."

Several officers rushed the building and began searching. Then, out of nowhere Kaze saw a small pair of red and white Air Max's approaching the driver's side of the pick-up truck! *Aww man! This some bullshit!,* he said to himself as he heard the door shut.

The pick-up truck started up! Clueless to his next move, Kaze panicked. His heart felt like it was trying to burst out of his chest as the truck began slowly backing out of the parking spot. That's when he noticed a thick metal pipe protruding from the undercarriage of the truck, and immediately wrapped his arms around it! Dragging his feet, and scraping up his heels, Kaze held on for dear life as the pick up truck pulled out of the parking lot and began driving through the city!

Minutes later, the truck stopped at a red light. Kaze felt he was far enough away from the projects, so he released the metal pipe and rolled from under the pickup truck. Kaze stood dusting himself off.

"Damn that was a close one", he said walking to the side walk as the female in the pickup truck and the other spectators looked at him with puzzled expressions on their faces.

Concerned if Real got caught or not, Kaze looked at his cell phone to dial Real's number but his phone was dead!
"Damn!"

He spotted a pay phone in front of a store and used it to dial Real's number.
"Yo?" Real answered.

Kaze was so relieved that Real didn't get caught he couldn't do anything but chuckle.

"Who the fuck is this?" Real asked thinking someone was playing on the phone.
"It's me nigga, Kamikaze!"
"Oh shit! I thought you got caught! I called your phone, but it went straight to voicemail!"
"My battery died!" Kaze replied.

Real was just as relieved to know they both got away. The two friends conversed and

laughed for a few minutes more before hanging up.

Once everything died down, Real and Kaze met up at Tadasia's apartment where Omar had the two bags of money waiting. He had gone to retrieve them out of the dumpster about an hour before they got there. Tadasia reported the Porsche stolen, and Real and Kaze had gone with her to get another one in another color. Real also explained what happened at his grandmother's house and asked his big sister if he could move in with her, of course she said yes.

CHAPTER 13

Trenton High had just let out and everyone's eyes were on the eggshell white four-door Porsche as Kaze pulled up in the overcrowded gas station directly across the street from the school.

"As soon as one of these hating ass niggas get on some bullshit, I'm gon' burn they asses up!" Kaze stated seriously.

He observed the displeased looks on the faces of some of the young men that stood around in several different crowds. He grabbed his black .380 semi-automatic handgun off his lap, cocked it back, and then tucked it inside of his front hoody pocket.

"Be easy, bruh, these niggas know better", Real assured calmly.

Real turned the volume on the radio all the way up, letting the song *'Million Dollar Baby'* by Max B scream through the speakers.

Real and Kaze both climbed out of the Porsche and began walking to the store connected to the gas station.

"What the fuck everybody looking at? What, y'all ain't never see two real niggas before?" Kaze bragged arrogantly looking at the several males and females that stood in the crowds staring at them.

This nigga shot the fuck out Real thought, chuckling before they walked inside the mini market.

Real and Kaze grabbed a flavored water out of the cooler, then headed to the counter to pay for their items.

"You got any single bills on you?" Real asked.

"Nah bruh, I ain't come outside with no money on me today", Kaze replied patting on his pockets.

Real pulled a knot of cash from out of his pocket and handed the tall Irish man behind the counter a twenty dollar bill. Just then two young females came sashaying through the door. One of the young females was brown skin with her hair wrapped up in a stylish

bun. The other had shiny chocolate skin, with long jet black silky hair that stopped near her lower back. "You might as well let him keep the change", the brown skin girl said as she approached Real.

Real stared at her while stuffing his change into his pocket.

"Oh so you ain't gon' let him keep it, huh?"
"Times are hard babes. I ain't rich", he replied smoothly as he licked his lips and smirked.

She looked Real up and down from head to toe, admiring the red and black Prada shoes that matched his jacket.
"Um hum, whateva. Anyway, what's your name?"
Real grabbed the charm on his rose gold chain, and held it up to her face. It read REAL in big bold letters flooded with diamonds. Because of all the bling, she had to slightly strain her eyes to see what it read. "Real, huh? That's cute! My name's Tia."

Kaze was just standing there watching Tia press up on his right-hand man, the whole time he knew what time it was.

"Bruh, I'm about to go sit in the car."

"Um hum sexy young boy. Where you think you going?" The chocolate young female asked him as she rushed behind Kaze.

Real and Tia both chuckled at the sight of her friend chasing behind Kaze then focused back on each other. "That's my friend, Kia. She shot the hell out ain't she?" Tia asked smiling.

Real nodded his head in agreement.

"So Real, what's your number? I know you got a phone."

"It's 609..."

Before Real could finish, he heard someone with a deep voice yell out.

"What the fuck is you doing all up in that li'l nigga face!"

Tia's eyes grew wide.

"Oh shit, that's my boyfriend", she whispered nervously.

She hesitantly walked over to her boyfriend, who was mean mugging Real. He was taller and bigger, but Real still wasn't intimidated.

"Baby, calm down! All he had asked me was did I have change for a 10 dollar bill."
"Aight, hurry up and come on before we miss the bus", he added as he gently grabbed her hand and led her out.

Real smirked at the comment. *This Crusty-the-Clown looking ass nigga calling me a li'l nigga and he's catching the bus,* Real thought as he exited behind them.

Real climbed inside the Porsche laughing.
"You got ole girl number?" Real asked Kaze.
"Yeah I got it. What's so funny though? I want to laugh too!"

Real nodded his head towards the bus stop, where Tia and her boyfriend were standing.

"That goofy ass nigga over there caught his girl drooling all over ya boy. Matter fact, stop at the bus stop real quick."

Real rolled the window down and hung half of his body out of it. Kaze slowed the Porsche to just in front of the bus stop.
"Come on babes! Hop in this Porsche and come take a ride with a boss! You look too good to be waiting on a bus stop", Real said charmingly as he motioned his hand for her to get inside the car.

The Porsche was so close to the bus stop, he could almost touch Tia. She wanted to hop in the Porsche with Real so bad, but was just too scared. She couldn't help but blush at Real's cocky attitude. Her boyfriend stood closely beside her, shooting him the 25 to life!

Real began laughing uncontrollably at how mad and stupid Tia's boyfriend looked before he slid his body back into the car. He rolled up the window as Kaze pressed down on the gas pedal, causing the tires to screech loudly as they sped off. All of the onlookers watched in

awe as the Porsche went flying down Chambers Street!

"You saw that stupid looking nigga face?" Real asked between laughs fastening his seat belt.

"Yeah I saw that clown", Kaze joined in the laughter as he glanced at Real.

Suddenly a mini van that was driving in front of them slammed on the brakes.

"Oh shit", Kaze exclaimed as he refocused on the road.

Kaze slammed his foot on the brake, but was going entirely too fast to stop without crashing into the back of the van. He quickly moved to the opposite side of the road, trying to avoid hitting the van, but to his surprise a 16 wheeler was approaching head on full speed beeping the horn! BEEP! BEEP! BEEP! "Aaahhh!" Real screamed scared to death closing his eyes.

Kaze managed to squeeze through the small space that was left between the two vehicles swiping the back of the Porsche against the

truck, causing him to swerve! Kaze burst out laughing.

"What the fuck you doing?! Praying?!"

Real slowly opened one eye, and a wave of relief came over him. He could've sworn his life was about to be done and over with! Real looked at Kaze like he was crazy as he shook his head and exhaled.

"Man you almost killed a nigga! Get me the hell out of this car! Let's go out the way and get some money!"

Kaze parked on Roselle Avenue, then he and Real got out. They both navigated through the big hole in the fence and began walking through the cut, which led them to the back of the deli that was on the next street.

"My bomb better still be back here", Kaze warned.

Kaze hoped that no one came behind the store to steal the work he had stashed. He began removing the boxes and crates near the back door while Real stood a few feet away patiently waiting for him.

Kaze grinned at the sight of the brown paper bag filled with crack, grabbing and stuffing it inside his Gucci pants pocket. Kaze and Real walked through the walkway on the side of store. Real's face lit up when he appeared in front of the store and saw a crowd of young men surrounding the dice game with wads of cash in their hands.

"Looks like I'm just in time."

"Lay 30 li'l nigga!" Uncle Chase yelled as a young hustler threw the dice against the red brick wall and rolled 1-2-3.

"Crap! I see why you act like you ain't hear me before you rolled the dice", Uncle Chase laughed.

Uncle Chase was a short and chubby brown skin older man with thick cornrows in his head that loved to gamble. Everyone in the 'hood knew whenever Uncle Chase was around it meant big money was involved.

"$30 ain't enough old head! Lay $60", Real upped the ante walking up to Uncle Chase as he swiped the dice from off the ground.
"Fuck them dice. Let's move the rest of this work!" Kaze told him, but Real ignored him.

"Whoever else wanna lay something just drop it on the ground!" Real announced.

The majority of the men placed their bets, then Real shook the dice and threw them against the wall, rolling 6-6-6.
"Trips! Kaze don't even trip bruh. I'm about to stick these niggas."

Kaze just shook his head as he turned around and began walking to the corner, where he was going to get his hustle on.

"I already see how this gon' play out. I ain't even gon' have to go in my pockets!" Real added chuckling as he picked the dice up.
"Same bet!" Uncle Chase said as he peeled off three twenty's from his roll of cash.
"If you laying a bet, drop it on the ground!" Real reminded him.

The same young men did as he instructed. Real threw the dice against the wall and rolled 2-2-6.

"Head!" Real shouted as he snapped his finger. "Y'all might as well save yaself some time and just give me all y'all money", he joked as he leaned down to pick up his winnings.

For a half hour straight, Real continued to throw stars or better, winning everyone's money and aggravating the shit out of Uncle Chase with his slick tongue. He was up $15 grand, when the tables turned and Real began craping out back to back. He was now down $9 grand and only had $500 dollars left in his pocket. He should've just walked away when he was winning. Real threw the dice against the wall and rolled 1-2-3.

"Crap catch 'em. I guess that li'l black skinny arm giving out on ya slick-talking ass huh?!" Uncle Chase yelled laughing.

Uncle Chase had a wad of cash in his hand and both of his front pockets were filled with Real's money. Real sighed out loud.
"This some bullshit!"

The look on Kaze's face said, *I don't know why you ain't listen to me!* It was like every time Real would warm up and throw a few heads, he would throw the same amount of craps and fall back into the hole he was trying to get out of.

Real placed another bet with Uncle Chase and a few of the other young men, dropping his last few hundred dollars on the ground when suddenly a masked man wearing a dark brown Champion hoody and a book bag strapped to his chest popped up from the side of the store.
"Get the fuck on the ground!"

The man pointed a black handgun at the crowd. Real and everyone else dove on the ground without even looking at the masked man. Uncle Chase took off running up the street as fast as he could! Not only did he

think the stick up kid was going to focus on the crowd instead of just one person running, he felt he worked too hard for his money to just be giving it up so easy. BLOW! BLOW! BLOW!

Three slugs chewed through Chase's lower back, causing him to drop the money he was holding in his hand and fall face first to the ground.
"Uhhgg!"

Uncle Chase started leaking like a faucet as he tried crawling away. The gunman ran up and stood over top of him. Hearing his footsteps, Uncle Chase slowly rolled over onto his back.
"Please don't kill me! Huh, take the money. I have plenty of money."

The masked man hurriedly pocketed the cash that was handed to him and the money that was on the ground. He then darted back through the side of the store fleeing the scene.

"Somebody call an ambulance", one of the young men yelled.

Everyone swiftly got up from the ground, some running to Uncle Chase's aid. Knowing that the police would be there at any moment, Real quickly got up from the ground and surveyed the area trying to spot Kaze, but he was nowhere to be found. He then ran off towards his sister's side of the projects, mad as hell. Real didn't give two fucks about Uncle Chase getting shot. Here he was, winning $15 grand and instead of quitting while he was ahead, he kept gambling and lost almost every dollar he had in his pocket.

Real spotted Kaze sitting in the Porsche parked in front of his sister's building.
"Damn, what took you so long to get up here?" Kaze asked as Real climbed in the car closing the door behind him.
"I was looking for you! I feel like shit right now man, I just lost almost 10 stacks!"
"I know whoever it was that just robbed Uncle Chase's fat ass happy as hell right now."
"Hell yeah they happy as hell. That's $35 grand", Real agreed wishing he was the one

that robbed him. "Nah, it wasn't $35 grand, it was $38 grand.", Kaze assured.
"How you know?"

Kaze reached under his seat, grabbed a black book bag, and threw it on Real's lap.
"That's how I know!"

A devilish grin slowly appeared on Kaze's face. Real's eyes grew wide at the sight of the book bag on his lap. He then looked back at Kaze's crazy ass! *This nigga terrible,* Real thought flabbergasted. He was just depressed about losing almost $10 grand, but was now sitting here with every dollar Uncle Chase had won on his lap!

"Thanks Kaze man! You shot the fuck out!"
"I ain't shot out. You was losing ya bread, so I got it back for you."
"I'm gon' just take what I lost."

Real opened the book bag and began counting the money.

"Take half of it. Matter fact, put it all in ya sister spot for right now because I don't feel like going to the crib", Kaze said.

Kaze felt his cell phone vibrating in his pocket.
"Yo, who dis?"
"This Kia."
"Oh shit, what's up babes, how you?"

Kaze looked at Real with his hand over the mouth piece.
"This that li'l chocolate bitch from the gas station", he whispered.

Kaze talked to Kia for about 10 minutes as he cruised through the town. She let him know that her girlfriend Tia wanted Real's cell number, so he gave it to her.

CHAPTER 14

"Awww, daddy fuck me good! Daddy fuck me harder!" China Doll moaned as Benji beat it up relentlessly from the back doggy style while pulling on her dark black hair and smacking her on her voluptuous yellow ass.

All you heard throughout the room was the sound of Benji's balls smacking against her fat and juicy soaking wet pussy lips as he pumped harder and harder.
"You want me to fuck you harder right? Huh? That's hard enough?" Benji asked, looking down at her ass cheeks jiggling as his hard rod went in and out. "Aww yes daddy. Right there! Oooh it feels so good. I'm about to cum!"

China Doll began moaning as she threw her ass back. Benji felt her pussy muscles tighten around his thickness and knew that he wasn't to far from climaxing along with her.
"This daddy pussy right?" He asked noticing the creamy thick cum that appeared on the shaft of his penis.

Suddenly the bedroom door was kicked open.
Several Federal agents rushed inside the
spacious bedroom with their guns drawn.
"FBI! Put your fucking hands up!"
China Doll snatched the red satin sheet from
off the king size bed to cover her nude body
as Benji, who was still on his knees, put his
hands up. An agent put Benji's hands behind
his back and slapped cuffs on his wrists.
China Doll was in shock.
"Baby what's going on?!"
"I don't know! But I'm gon' call you once I get
where I'm going."

The agent snatched him off the bed and
escorted Benji out of the house.

After the Feds came through and snatched
Benji from the streets, the 'hood hadn't been
the same. There was only bullshit coke
floating around, and the organized structure
Benji built and maintained in the 'hood was
slowly falling apart. It was as if everyone was
out for self.

Real and Kaze, who were both feeling like they had lost a piece of themselves since Benji's arrest, stood in front of the deli trying to figure out where they were going to get some work.

"Man, where in the hell we gon' get some work from?" Real asked.

They hadn't moved coke in two whole weeks. Seeing all that paper pass by and being unable to get it had him sick to his stomach.

"That fat ass nigga Roe got some coke", Kaze responded.

Kaze took a deep pull on his blunt of purple haze while he glanced at the cars riding by.

"Man, I'm talking about some Grade A shit. Nobody want that coke that been stepped on a hundred times that Roe be selling."
"Fuck it then we just gon' start robbing everybody who selling weight in the City."
"Nah, we can't do that", Real said.
"Well, we gon' have to do something because I refuse to be broke again!"

Just then, a pink DB9 Aston Martin with dark tinted windows pulled up in front of the store and parked. They both watched with wide lustful eyes as the slanted eyed exotic looking young lady got out of the car. Her silky jet black wavy hair stopped near her lower back, and her luscious pink lips were full. She wore an all black short sleeved body suit that complimented every single curve on her voluptuous petite frame.

"Real", she called as she approached him and Kaze.
She noticed the letters that were engraved in the rose gold charm on his chain. She knew exactly who Real was because Benji gave her a description of him in the letter he wrote her.

Real and Kaze looked at each other at the same time, and then looked back at the exotic-looking creature. She noticed the puzzled look on Real's face.
"Benji sent me to come out here and find you. He got something he want you to see. I

would've called, but he told me not to talk over the phone."

Everything the lady just said made sense, but Real was still a little suspicious. Benji always told him to never let a female's beauty blind you. Plus, he knew it was a possibility that he could get wrapped up in whatever it was the Feds snatched Benji up for, so he definitely had to be on point.

"Who you?" Real asked.

"I'm China Doll, Benji's wifey."

China Doll proudly showed the tattoo of Benji's face on a hundred dollar bill on her forearm. Benji made sure to keep her far away from the 'hood. No one ever saw her or even knew Benji had a wifey. His relationship with China Doll was probably the only thing he didn't show off or brag about.

"Hurry up and get in the car", she demanded as she walked back to the stylish vehicle.

Real and Kaze walked toward the car.

"Now hold up. I said Real, not Real and his sidekick!" China Doll said looking at Kaze before getting inside the car.

Who the fuck she think she talking to? Kaze said to himself as he stopping in his tracks and twisted up his face. Real noticed the disturbed look on his righthand man's face.

"Don't even trip bruh. I'll be right back in a few minutes. Wait in front of my sister's building for me."

Kaze gained his composure and nodded his head in agreement. Real got inside the car, and China Doll pulled off.

"So what's going on with big bruh? How's he doing?"

"He's doing aight. They charged him with serving a Federal Informant and had him under a six month wire tap investigation."

Real swallowed hard, it felt like his heart skipped a beat as he began thinking about all the conversations that he and Benji had over the phone.

"Yeah? They got him on wire taps?" Real said, hoping that he had heard incorrectly.

"Um huh, that's what he said."

"So how much time is he facing?"

"He doesn't know yet, but I'm sure he'll find out once he talks to his lawyer", she told him as she gently pressed her foot on the brake, stopping at a red light.

"Grab that letter from the glove compartment. It's from Benji." Real reached for the letter, taking it out the already opened envelope. He began reading.

Li'l Bro, what's good?!

I don't want to hold you up for too long, so I'm gon' get straight to the point. I need you to get rid of two of them things for me, and go collect 30 from Roe and that other 30 grand from my nigga Snake Eyes. Once everything's everything, hit my lady with the bread.

The hood is yours!

P.S. Real niggaz make shit happen.

After Real read the letter, he looked at China Doll.

"Where the work at?"

"It's at my house", China Doll replied.

"Let's go get it."

China Doll drove to her house, grabbed the coke for Real, and then dropped him off in front of his sister's building.

"Aight, I'm gon' call you as soon as I put everything together."

"Be careful out here", China Doll warned.

"Oh, don't worry. I will!" Real stated as he got out of the car.

Real watched as the Aston Martin drove out of the parking lot. He noticed that Kaze was sitting on the bench in front of the building so he began walking towards him.

"Oh shit, there he go!" Kaze said playfully as Real approached him.

"Read this, man."

Real handed Kaze the letter. Kaze read the letter and frowned.

"I thought Roe's fat fake ass was doing his own thing."

One thing Kaze couldn't stand was a fronting ass nigga. Real chuckled and shook his head.

"Man you know how muhfuckas is."

"I know niggas better start having that bread. Bitch the 'hood is ours!" Kaze said.

Real and Kaze discussed how they were going to go about handling everything. Afterwards, they went to the trap house, cooked up the work, and began supplying the whole 'hood.

About The Author

Carde'l was born and raised in Trenton, New Jersey. A natural born writer, Carde'l is an inspiring life-long writer whose homegrown fiction keeps you on the edge of your seat! He hopes that the *Diamond in the Dirt* book series does not disappoint. Carde'l is the author of *Cold World* and is in the process of writing more thought-provoking works of fiction that celebrate the avenues of adversity which address the isolated issues we encounter in urban communities. His hope is to raise consciousness and awareness and to inspire readers from all backgrounds. He was inspired to write *Diamond in the Dirt* after witnessing many young men in the community so easily influenced by their peers. He hopes you will continue to support him in his effort to reach people by reading all his titles including *Cold World* which can be found on amazon.com.

Diamond in the Dirt 2 **and** *Cold World* **out now!**

CARDE'L

Book cover designed by Justin Q Young
Book editing by Tiffany Horn

Published by Richard Jenkins for BLOCK STAR BOOKS

Printed in the United States of America

Carde'l contact info: *cardelunlimited@gmail.com*
Instagram: @CARD_E_L
Twitter: @CardelWrites
website: blockstar.blog

Diamond in the Dirt

By Carde'l